A
Piney Mountain
Holiday

by

Mia Frazier

PRESS

A Piney Mountain Holiday is a work of fiction. Names, characters, places, and incidents are either products of the author's imagination or are used fictitiously. Any resemblance to actual events, businesses, locales, or persons, living or dead, is entirely coincidental.

2021 Bleau Press

ISBN 978-1-951796-08-2 (paperback)
ISBN 978-1-951796-09-9 (ebook)

Illustrations by David North

A
Piney Mountain
Holiday

A Very Yeti Christmas

Lisa

It shouldn't be sleeting. Like all residents of Piney Mountain, I think of my weather.gov app as an iPhone Bible sent directly from the Heavens. When I left Roanoke, there only was a 50% chance of light rain and an overnight low of 35.

NOAA must have missed the memo the karma gods have decided to flash-freeze the mountain before we can be smogged out by the new factory.

My sister, Lauren, continues talking through my car speakers as I pull onto some frozen mud off the side of the road. There's no way to stop her, and around the middle of her lecture about the magical powers of glow lotion and Caribbean vacations and sweaty sex, she starts to sound like a disgruntled self-help god.

I look up the back road leading to Piney Falls. It ends right in the middle of an ominous-looking cloud that's currently spitting sleet into my windshield. So Caribbean vacations and sweaty sex are probably even farther than usual from my mind tonight.

"I have to go," I say again. Since the cell tower on this side of the mountain was struck by lightning in September, my phone's been losing signal around the next couple curves in the road, anyway.

The bolt came just after news the wilderness refuge around our mountain will be flattened, its waterfall filled in at the behest of Heslein Incorporated, LLC. It's a sick holiday magic trick; the child labor on Heslein's plastics come from China, their taxes stay in a bank account in Belize, and the pollution from the processing plant will come out right here in Virginia.

Lauren keeps talking, reiterating the concern she's had since Thanksgiving that I'm not glowy enough. And that, combined with my usual Friday night activities—or lack of Friday night activities—almost guarantees I'll be single and cursed to decorate the homes of Virginia's newlyweds for the rest of my existence. I try to tell Lauren this isn't such a bad fate; newlyweds like to redecorate.

"You should be traveling," she says. "Going out to dinners. That kind of thing. All this stress is bad for your skin tone." Lauren's 5'8, doesn't experience stress, and is constantly glowy, apparently the result of lots of sweaty sex and gallons of daily carrot juice.

I drum through the hourly forecast on my phone as she threatens to send me more of her glow lotion and some tooth-whitening strips, because apparently my teeth are getting kind of dingy, too. Where my sister's hydraulic car elevators and helipads, I'm more African mudcloth and seagrass—simple, blendable, pretty much made of neutrals. Not meant for date shopping in my thirties in greater Appalachia, in other words. Or probably anywhere else.

I remind her of my current location on the side of the road and reiterate the difficulty of my situation—trying to save the town's wilderness refuge with the cash I made renovating a banquet hall in hideous baby blues last month. It's possible we both should have seen this coming; there's only so much baby blue a person can handle before skin tone starts to suffer.

"You're still doing it?" Lauren demands, but she's talking about Heslein, not about the blues.

"I'm on the city council."

Lauren makes a sound like her parrot, Huntley, when he regurgitates a banana. She started making this noise when I was first drafted to the town council by Mayor Gliel about a year ago. But until Heslein invaded in August, my most ambitious project was the installation of a new crosswalk sign.

I repeat *serenity* in my mind (The irony of being assigned 'serenity' as a meditation mantra isn't lost on me.), my knuckles white on the steering wheel as I catch Lauren up on tonight's meeting in Roanoke, during which Thomas Eckert, esquire charged us $600 to say that the EPA only regulates air, water, and noise pollution in metro areas over 100,000 people. Piney Falls could possibly reach 150 by 2025 if the Martins keep reproducing like pantry moths.

Now Heslein's turning the tables, contracting some even pricier lawyer to sue *us* for holding up a potential thirteen million in profits since our protest stopped them from breaking ground before the new year.

Lauren, true to form, is undaunted from her mission. "You should be going out," she repeats. "With non-mountain people. *Dating*."

"This isn't a good time," I tell her.

Lauren sighs like Huntley when he's imitating Dad's Harley. "You're getting nasal again. You sound like a hyena." This, from someone who sounds like a hyperventilating African Grey.

Then she starts in on her yoga speech, the one insisting I'll be more glowy and more bendy and attract more hot males with whom to have sweaty sex and get even more glowy and bendy, if I just trade city council meetings for yoga.

I make appropriate sounds of agreement, but I should have earned plenty of good karma tonight by resisting the urge to smother Thomas Eckert with one of his pretentious, oh-so-beige throw pillows.

"I'm on the side of the road in an ice storm," I reiterate.

There's a pause at the other end of the line. "An ice storm? You're alone?" I'm pretty sure Lauren doesn't understand the concept; she has a male someone she can call for any life situation, from ants in her kitchen to a service light in her car to a last-minute accountant.

"Where are you?" she asks.

"The back road." It's not even marked at the bottom of the mountain. That's why we call it "the back road."

"I'm okay," I add. My good karma should be hitting me any second now. "I'm almost home," I lie.

After a quick reminder to juice only organic carrots (for pesticide-free, optimal glowiness), Lauren hangs up, and I turn my car's radio to a soothing classical station.

My tires crunch loudly over the frozen mud as I try to get some traction to launch my Focus up the hill and face the sleet head on. *I can do this*, I tell myself, just in case subliminal suggestions really work, and since I'm pretty sure I'm flunking *serenity* right now. But the universe sends good things to people who do good things, and all that, and I'm overdue for some seriously good karma.

The haunting, unreasonably loud oboe solo from Dvorjak's "Noon Witch" blares through the speakers as my car's back wheels squeal and my hood spins past a row of evergreens.

The car slides backwards, Dvorjak muffled by the crunching of ice under the tires as I fall back into the wilderness refuge at the base of the mountain.

2

When I get my bearings again, my pulse is faster than the Dvorjak oboe, and my arms hurt from bracing against the steering wheel. But thank the karma gods the branch was there to catch me.

I reach out to touch the end that extends through my windshield, its tip sharpened in an ominous point. If Lauren had her way, there probably would have been a man sitting in my passenger seat on a Friday night, and he would have been staked in the heart like a vampire with really bad karma.

I force my eyes to focus on where my passenger branch protrudes from a downed tree. Then I twist to look back at where I think the road is. All I can see is sleet.

I suck in some deep breaths to slow my pulse and try

to summon good energy, but it's not easy to channel chi through an open forest. Better the branch stop me, I guess, than the giant spruce a few feet ahead that would have crunched me into a yellow Focus pancake. And with the freak lightning storm and the weater.gov-defying icing at 35 degrees, I should at least be able to rest in peace knowing that, when my car's finally found after the spring thaw and my body is bear poo fertilizing the new saplings, it was all the work of a higher power.

I turn off the engine to conserve gas, and a chill sets in right away, a cold that seeps deep into my bones and makes me reconsider Lauren's suggestion of a Caribbean vacation.

I take inventory of my situation. My phone's lost service, and the only food I have with me is a binder full of chocolate bars from my neighbor's basketball camp fundraiser. I remind myself I'm still serene—because there's something to be said for faking it—and decide to leave the radio on classical, typing an SOS text to Mayor Gliel in case my phone catches a signal long enough to send it. Then I curl up to conserve warmth until someone drives by. By the forest, that is, in the middle of the night. My fingers twinge as I set my phone back in its cup holder.

Somewhere in the middle of Tchaikovsky, the phone beeps to let me know the battery's low, and I find the SOS message still in my outbox. A cursory glance around the backseat—currently full of bathroom designs—yields no better windshield protector than a light jacket, and I start the car again, carefully wedging the fabric between the glass shards of the windshield. Mayor Gliel has few cabins on this side of the mountain, but they're only rented during the summers, and I don't have enough candy bars to hibernate.

My headlights flash back on when I turn the key, and cold air blasts through the vents.

Then something about a snowdrift on the other side of the spruce catches my eye, and whatever wasn't frozen in me before freezes now. I snatch a pair of prescription sunglasses from my visor and squint into the headlights. The snow drift comes into focus. It has legs. And is almost certainly a yeti.

I turn down the volume on the radio in case yeti are attracted to classical music like plants or babies are. I must have hit my head somewhere between the road and the tree branch. Was it yeti that frequent the mountains of Virginia, or wendigos? Ever since that episode of *Supernatural* Lauren had me watch over Thanksgiving, I've been having sporadic nightmares about the souls of my ancestors trapped in the bodies of eternal cannibals who go in search of victims in the wilderness every seven years.

Or maybe it was fourteen. Whichever, if ever there were a year for a wendigo near the future Heslein site, this would be it.

The wendigo falters in the snow. I push my sunglasses up on my nose. It's not very fast for a wendigo, but then, it probably hasn't been able to find any victims on this side of the mountain for a while. Maybe hunger's weakened it. I kill the volume on the radio, cutting off something appropriately Copland.

When the wendigo pushes himself back up onto his feet, his cream-colored coat glistens in the headlights. So maybe a yeti, then. Yeti are cream-colored, I think.

I dig my fingers under my hair but don't feel any bumps as I watch the yeti lumber forward. Yes, yeti *lumber*. That sounds right. So it's almost definitely not a wendigo. I'm pretty sure those leap between trees, anyway, if *Supernatural* can be trusted.

My pulse hammers in my temples, and I reach for my only hope at self-defense, the binder full of Snickers, as Bigfoot approaches the front of my car.

I shift into reverse and try the gas. The car spins directly sideways, anchored by the branch. It comes to a stop with the yeti at my front window. I beep my horn. You know, in case that might change something.

He knocks on the glass. And I'm sure, then, when I see his face, that the wreck and the factory and the lawsuit are the least of my problems.

As I gaze into the eyes of the yeti through the corrective lens of my sunglasses and the not-so-safety glass of my car window, I imagine I'm having one of those spiritual experiences my Native American heritage—all sixteenth of it—is supposed to bring about to lead me into the afterlife. And I know this because, dreadlocks and lumbering and all, I'm attracted to a yeti.

3

So my spiritual guide looks like a hot yeti, and my great journey's to his cabin instead of to the afterlife. Under different circumstances, I'd probably be thrilled to follow an attractive man wearing a coat that makes him look like Bigfoot to his warm cabin on a cold, icy night. Or at least everything but the Bigfoot part. But then, under different circumstances, I probably wouldn't find anyone with dreadlocks covering his torso attractive. Maybe Lauren's right and my dating life really has reached a critical point in having brought on such elaborate and hairy hallucinations.

The furry coat's around me now, and I'm lumbering very much like a yeti might through the layers of leaves and snow. I duck as an ice-coated branch snags my hair. The snow's soaked all the way through my pumps.

I risk a glance at my rescuer as we get closer to the cabin. In just a sweater now, he's like an attractive ghost of under-insulated Christmas. Little beads of snow stick to his shoulders like sparkly dandruff and glisten under the porch light.

A wall of warmth hits me when he opens the door, and I quickly slip off my pumps and shed the yeti coat into a hall closet, where it must have been left by a very old model of Gliel. Then I head for the red rug I advised our color-insensible mayor not to position so close to the fireplace.

My spiritual guide stays several paces away. He's been looking at me like *I* was the yeti since he opened my car door—which I really thought I'd locked—and some Snickers fell out of my self-defense binder. Maybe I should have done more explaining and less curling up in preparation to kick. Maybe I should have taken off my sunglasses. Hindsight in these situations is always 20/20.

"You're sure you're not hurt," he repeats. His voice is soft and slow, like he's talking to a lost kitten or a lunatic.

I've answered this already, of course, but it's not easy to articulate when you're facing Bigfoot.

I tell him I'm fine, but the side of my face farthest from the fire hasn't thawed yet, and I probably look like one of those bad Botox cases from Virginia Beach.

He shifts his weight but doesn't leave the doorway. He still looks like he's deciding whether to flee. Whether *he* should flee. I probably shouldn't have screamed. Maybe I shouldn't have mentioned yeti after that, either, in my apology.

"And you were on the road...why were you on the road?" he asks. His eyebrows are bunched together like hibernating wooly worms. This was the look, ironically, that made me wish I'd given more thought to things like glow lotion and tooth-whitening strips. Lauren might be right about my Friday nights, instant yeti attraction notwithstanding.

I sniff. The snot glacier in my nose is finally starting to melt. "Business," I tell him.

"What kind of...I'm sorry." He raises his palms in front of his chest. "That's another personal question."

In my adrenaline-powered post-crash state, I guess I took releasing my name as a personal question and made it clear I wouldn't release personal information to yeti-dressed men who frequent otherwise abandoned mountainsides. But the suspicion obviously faded quickly enough; something about my reluctant spiritual guide gives me the impression of solidity, of being someone you can trust.

Lauren, of course, would be quick to diagnose this as a symptom of my lack of a dating life, too, being shaken off balance so easily by the appearance of a yeti-dressed stranger in the woods. And rationally, more alarm bells probably should be going off; my rescuer fits the serial killer MO—perfect teeth, thick, almost black hair, a killer smile. Like the kind of killer who sneaks into abandoned cabins in the middle of nowhere, you know, wandering out into the wilderness only when it's time to find a new victim. Kind of like a wendigo, I think, except those don't need cabins since they build underground lairs in which to store their victims for optimal freshness.

He goes over same questions as before, the *Are you warm enough*'s and the *Are you sure you didn't hit your head*'s. I respond by quizzing him about his cabin rental and his hairy choice of outerwear.

"And your name," I prompt when I've run out of questions.

"Kurt Boxler."

It sounds familiar for some reason, and I stretch my legs out in front of me, letting my body sink down into the rug. *Boxler*. It reminds me of cuddly Boxers with their scrunchy faces and their sweet affinity for bacon.

"And you have an ID?" Not that I'd know if Kurt Boxler were a prolific serial killer just by his name. I mean, I'm sure he'd have another name, probably Chopper someone or something Slasher. His chest looks like he'd be good at chopping and slashing.

He hands me a driver's license. I study his height and weight description and note that he doesn't wear glasses or contacts. He's an organ donor, of course. These are the kinds of things you check, apparently, after a semi-spiritual experience in the wilderness.

I give the license back to him, and he says something about a charger in the bedroom for my phone. I takes me a second to get up and follow him, but even if he were a serial killer, I'm pretty sure he wouldn't kill me in the bedroom. The furniture's so much more balanced here, and blood stains would clash with the blue.

Once we're through the door, he takes the phone from my hand and places it on a black pad on the windowsill. "It's a solar charger," he explains. "You set it here, and..."

"But it's dark."

"Right." He's talking slowly again, and my head's starting to feel funny. "It charged during the day. It sort of stores it."

As the yeti-man explains the benefits of solar charging in the wilderness, I wonder if I should write down any of the symptoms I'm experiencing to report to my doctor. It's probably whiplash, though it's possible there's some hormonal component, too. But I'm much too young for menopause. Well, maybe not *much*. Maybe it has something to do with the lightning strike energy on this side of the mountain. It does feel kind of like lightning, and maybe a little like the ravioli I had for dinner was bad.

Kurt's voice pulls me from my thoughts on food poisoning.

"The shower," he's saying now, laying out some dry clothes for me along the foot of the bed. "You just have to flip the switch on the side of the tub."

I look down. My suit jacket and shell are completely soaked through from when I launched out of the car, revealing a lumpy bra circa the late 1990's.

I avoid looking in the mirror when the yeti man leaves me to it, promising to make us some dinner.

4

I lean back under the spray of the shower and imagine all my stress being steamed out my pores. I was so focused on not smothering the lawyer in Roanoke with his throw pillows, I was probably even less prepared than usual for a wreck and a yeti encounter tonight.

My head's still buzzing, and I focus on taking deep breaths as I rinse out Kurt's shampoo. It's a spicy, woodsy scent that makes me think of fireplaces and yeti. Or at least of pinecones. These are the kinds smells that are meant to lure you into a false sense of complacency regarding holiday craziness, though, like warm earth tones and suede at a neo-Nazi headquarters.

Not that there's anything I can do about the potential danger of my situation; I'm here at least until a wrecker can get to me. The way I see it, this steamy bathroom is either my incredible karma, with a handsome stranger on the other side of the door cooking our dinner, or a scene from a Steven King movie, trapped with a psychopathic serial killer who's probably getting ready to cook *me*.

When I slip on his sweatpants and Boston College hoodie, I settle on the former. Soft fabric psychology must really work. I pull on the socks he left for me, too, before padding over to my cell phone.

It starts up slowly, evidently still cold despite being energized by the magnetic field over the solar charger, and displays two missed calls from Mayor Gliel and one from Lauren. Since I'm in Gliel's cabin, I decide confirming the handsome stranger who brought me here isn't a serial killer is more important than another lecture about glow lotion.

Gliel picks up on the first ring. "You're all right?" he asks. "Adam couldn't get a clear read on your GPS. Lisa? Can you hear me? It's saying you're somewhere in the forest on the East side of the mountain. I have a cabin open on the..."

Gliel's been prone to babbling since the Heslein business started. Before the factory threat, he served as Piney Falls' mayor for over twenty years without incident. He's been trying to gracefully retire for most of the last decade, but no one else would volunteer, and our town's veteran psychic predicted his would be a violent retirement.

"Lisa?" he repeats, his voice sounding more croaky.

Maybe it's my growing headache, but Gliel's always reminded me a bit of a bullfrog—the sympathetic type, you know, always sort of lost and hopping through the Piney Mountain wilderness. I tried to include soothing sea greens in his living room, but it's possible I went a little overboard.

Knowing all the greens in the world couldn't soothe him with the Heslein business, I wouldn't have texted him about my wreck if he weren't the only person I know with numbers for the entire town and most of the emergency services in Virginia in his contacts.

So I explain my situation as calmly as I can through the "safe in a warm cabin" part, then casually inquire if the cabin is, in fact, safe, properly rented and not broken into by some deranged mountain man who just happens to own cozy sweatpants and Christmassy shampoo.

"Kurt's...there," Gliel says when I finish.

"And he's okay?" I ask. My temples twinge when the line goes quiet. "Gliel?"

"Oh, yeah," he says. "Of course he's okay. You were coming from the meeting in the city, weren't you?"

"Uh huh." I fiddle with the cord to the blinds. Maybe he means Kurt's self-sufficient, and so okay himself in an ice storm, but not necessarily okay for others, like an orca at great depths.

"I feel awful you're going through this," Gliel says, and he does sound pretty awful.

He keeps talking, and I look out the window as the porch light catches the sleet. This is what the refuge always looks like just before Christmastime, a silent, shimmering expanse of fresh snow and icicles. These woods are full of so many stories, I know, that start a little like this one, with someone being rescued and spending the night in a stranger's cabin. The preserve is like a buffer between Piney Falls and the outside world, exactly the same as it was before Roanoke, Radford, and all the other towns around the mountain started to write their own stories.

"I'm all right," I repeat.

Gliel listens quietly to my post-wreck positivity, but I can tell he's picking his fingernails again. He's had bloody nail beds for the last few months.

"You know, you're running yourself a little ragged," he says when I finish with the feigned calm and Heslein optimism. "Maybe it's time for a vacation."

"A vacation?"

He sighs. "I think you're beat. For now," he clarifies. "For now, I think you should take a break."

But Gliel knows a break would mean a permit, and a permit would mean the end of the Piney Mountain wilderness area, and that would mean the end of Piney Falls as we know it. The pressure in my head shifts behind my eyes, and I feel tears starting to well up. They're overdue, probably, after months of Heslein and then the beige-pillowed lawyer and the wreck.

Gliel clears his throat and goes back to his mayor voice. "There's a big tree down by the pass, and Adam says we can't even get a wrecker out there till morning."

"Really, I'm fine," I tell him. I hear movement in the kitchen and lower my voice. But at worst, I'm stranded with a responsible serial killer who pays for his cabins.

My phone beeps to let me know its battery's low as Gliel gives me unnecessary instructions about firewood and the thermostat I've been able to work since I started delivering girl scout cookies here at age seven. He sounds like he's progressed to high-stress scalp-picking mode now.

"And Kurt, he's here on private business," he adds. "I mean, he's an out-of-towner, you know, so he doesn't need to be in the thick of everything."

"Uh huh." As though we might need any more reasons for tourists not to visit the future site of the orange foam swamp. If Heslein's plan goes through, these woods will quickly be cleared for low-rent housing for the factory's employees. My hand twinges, probably looking to smother someone with a beige throw pillow. It's lucky there aren't any here. Tonight, it's possible I'm as dangerous as anyone I might meet in these woods other than a real yeti.

"And you'll be there?" Gliel asks, like I might leave the warm cabin and try my hand at winter camping. "I mean, you're comfortable?"

I look down at Kurt's pajamas. "Sure," I say. "Of course." We mountain dwellers are hardy folk.

*   *

"Tell me you haven't moved anything." Lauren's made Huntley's banana regurgitation sound twice since she answered her phone.

I return my ear to the solar pad charging my iPhone—and, with it, probably the left side of my brain.

"Of course not," I say.

Lauren hasn't let me forget about rearranging my last date's living room. But that was over a year ago, and his house had feng shui-crushing poison arrows everywhere. And anyway, that wasn't why we stopped seeing each other. The real problem was the giant swordfish....a for real, very dead swordfish nailed to a plank of wood on his living room wall like a spiny Jesus on the cross. No one can forge a meaningful relationship with someone who nails a dead swordfish over his sofa.

"This guy who found you," Lauren continues. "Is he hot?" Not *Is he unarmed?* or *Is he a Westboro Baptist Church member?* or *Does he deal hard drugs?* Lauren has her priorities.

I mumble something noncommittal that evidently gives Lauren all the information she needs.

"What are you wearing?" she asks.

I glance down at Kurt's sweatpants. "It doesn't matter," I tell her, then, "nothing inappropriate." For a pajama party, anyway. The fact that I'm even considering the appropriateness of my attire now convinces me I'm having some sort of a solar experience from keeping my head on the charger for too long.

Lauren snorts in a way that, if it came from Huntley, would make her call the vet. "It matters," she says. "You're trapped with a hot guy in a cabin with a fire overnight."

How she inferred the fire, I don't know. Lauren's imagination runs wild where men are concerned.

"Lisa? Am I speakerphone? Trust me, it matters."

"Uh huh." I turn down the volume on my phone, carrying it with me as I go sit on the bed and glance at an open folder on the nightstand—just glance, so I'm not really cheating on my rule not to exchange personal information with the stranger whose bedroom I'm in. The folder's open to landscape photos of the waterfall. They're good pictures, and I get a sense of okayness. It must mean Kurt's a photographer, which I assume are much less dangerous than, say, yeti.

"Lisa? Can you hear me? This is the clearest sign the universe could possibly give you that you have its permission to stop talking to lawyers and playing city council designer and, you know, have *fun*. Talk to people. People who don't live on the mountain. Go *out*."

"Out," I echo to indicate I'm still listening.

"And you still haven't changed your profile picture."

"Right." A few weeks ago, I promised Lauren I'd change my Facebook profile to something Christmassy to incite cuddling instincts and visions of sugarplums and subliminal libido boosters in my profile viewers. Apparently, my sister hasn't noticed I only have forty Facebook friends, most of whom are members of the Piney Falls knitting club.

"*A puking tree*," she whines.

"Mmm." I would have thought trees would be better for libido, being phallic and all. And my profile picture's iconic, in its way. It's our town logo, a historic tree from the preserve with our waterfall. And is definitely not puking.

"You know, your stress levels..." And as she launches into some Lauren-style explanation of how getting off the mountain will boost my immunity and ultimately prevent future breakouts, I have to admit my quacky sister might not be completely off the mark on this one. My shamanistic experience was a hot guy dressed up like a yeti; I'm not sure what a clearer sign from the universe that I should be getting out more would look like.

When I hear movement outside the bedroom door, I switch the phone off speaker.

"Lisa?" she asks.

"Gotcha. The flu's gonna be bad this year." And,

according to Lauren, I should do whatever I can to hook up with the only stranger on the mountain to boost my immunity and make me forget about puking tree preservation.

"And it will help your karma," Lauren adds, obviously grasping at straws now.

"My karma's great," I tell her. There's a soft knock on the door. "Better than great," I say. "I've been saving up."

5

Something about sharing dinner with a handsome stranger—even though it was a just a peanut butter and jelly sandwich and some canned tomato soup—gives me a burst of energy by mid-evening. It's that lingering feeling of uncertainty, I think, that's reserved for first dates, minor concussive injuries, and being trapped in snowed-in cabins with potential serial killers.

Now Kurt's making hot chocolate, remaining concussion-level charming. But serial killers are always charming. Lauren would say this kind of assessment is a big part of the reason I can't date properly, especially around the holidays. Because there's something about spiked cider and icy roads and families that brings out the serial killer in the best of us.

"Nutmeg?" he asks. "I found some in the pantry."

"I'm allergic," I say, then think better of it. Anaphylactic reactions are personal information. And allergies are so unattractive. "Intolerant," I correct. "Actually, I just really don't like it."

He looks at me for a second before disappearing back into the kitchen. I'm starting to think now that his eyes look more like hot chocolate than like a demonic possession in *Supernatural*, and I can't help but wonder what kinds of people he's used to eating dinner with. Our conversation's been light, covering easy topics far from romantic relationships, but he probably has someone who looks more like Lauren on call for his Friday nights at home.

"What about cinnamon?" he asks.

I confirm my cinnamon tolerance, and he emerges a minute later carrying two steaming mugs of cocoa. When he takes a seat on the cushion next to mine, the smell of peppermint zum bar and pinecone shampoo waft over me with the warmth of the fire.

He hands me a mug, one of the old blue ones that's been here as long as I can remember. "So it's not a very common allergy, is it?" he asks. "Nutmeg?"

I sniff but detect no nutmeg. Maybe my nose is overwhelmed, too, though, by the hot guy next to me who smells like a peppermint pinecone.

"And that's not a personal question," he adds, "because it's directed at the general population of allergy sufferers."

I smile as I blow across the surface of the hot chocolate. This man could pull a smile even from Lucy Lowens. "I don't know," I tell him. "They test for it, though." Nutmeg allergy is just one of those things you think can't happen to you, like this, now. "And I'm only intolerant," I remind him.

He nods and takes a sip from his mug, the steam rising up over his face. "I haven't made hot cocoa in a while. *Lisa*," he adds.

Which I guess I neglected to tell him until midway through our dinner. I wonder what kind of person allows someone into their cabin without knowing their name. I demanded a government-issued ID, and it's not even my cabin.

"Kurt," I return. Which sounds a lot better than "yeti." Kurt also looks much nicer than a yeti in the firelight.

I lean back against the cushions as I sip the cocoa. It tastes like a melted Dove bar, but without any of the nasty syrups Lauren's teaching me to shun, a kind of pure sin done right.

"I might have used too much cinnamon," Kurt warns me.

As the liquid slides down my throat, warmth spreads across my chest. It feels like hope and Christmas and everything else I've been missing out on this year with the lawsuit and the orange foam threat and all the discord among the knitting club.

Kurt shifts on the sofa next to me. When he smiles, he looks even yummier than a Dove bar. It's possible the whiplash has shaken loose an inappropriate level of hormones in my brain. That, or this is the most pleasant coma in the history of intra-cranial injuries.

Kurt tells me about how he started subbing coconut milk in the cocoa for his little sister, Hannah, because she's lactose intolerant, and about reading her Dr. Seuss books when she couldn't sleep. He felt responsible for her eating a bendy straw when she was little and has spoiled her ever since.

"I never thought about it, but I always added a lot of vanilla," he says. "I hope it didn't do anything bad to her. The alcohol in it. I mean, it probably did. She'll only drink things that taste like coconut or fruit now. It's probably some weird addiction that's going to mess with her work."

"What does she do?"

"She's a lawyer."

"Ouch," I say, because apparently the cocoa's also melted away the last of my verbal filters.

He nods. "Yeah, it's stressful for her, I think. She's been wanting to have a baby recently, and the long hours are hard on her."

We talk for a while about family, and I apparently forget my rule about exchanging personal information. I tell Kurt about Lauren's nutritionist weirdness, which somehow segues into my Uncle Jim and something about a family history of kidney stones. Not quite as cute as Hannah's bendy straws and coconut drinks. The fire pops, and Kurt gets up and pokes at a log.

You'd think my body would be exhausted from the crash and that my mind would have shut off by now, but it feels like energy's sort of buzzing through me. I don't know how much time passes as our conversation turns to other subjects and the ice pelting the windows turns to fat, silent flakes of snow.

Probably due to the alcohol content of the vanilla extract in the cocoa, at some point, I inquire about the pictures on Kurt's nightstand and, probably due to the general defenselessness that infects our psyches around the holiday season, he acknowledges he's here on consulting work.

'Consulting' is so vague, it could be anything, and I imagine him traveling the world, taking beautiful pictures and sampling odd cuisines like those nomadic backpackers or the people who live in vans who make youtube channels.

"I've been...reconsidering it, I guess you'd say, lately," he says. "My work's in the city—it's L.A. usually—and it's not really what I thought it would be back when I got started. I've moved around a lot. What about you?"

I tell him the usual boring story—that I'm from the mountain and came home after school, that I love it and am happiest here but that Gliel's probably right about it being too long since I've taken a vacation. I want to pretend my roots haven't started rotting these last several months fighting Heslein. Even if just for a night, I almost wish I could see myself as someone different altogether— as a Lauren, maybe, in a dress instead of sweats, the kind of woman someone like Kurt might have dinner with intentionally.

Kurt asks me more about the area, and I tell him about everything but the imminent plastics factory—the pageant and the Christmas tree lighting, the sledding and the parties and the Bakeoff.

"I wish I had someplace like that," he says when I've finished. "Even in the suburbs, it's just...not like that."

So we talk about funny HOA regulations and rooftop decorations, and at some point, I realize the fire's almost burned out. It's well past midnight, and I haven't noticed the too-warm reds surrounding us for hours.

"I think I'd better...." I start. "I didn't know it was so late." I want to think it's just the cocoa equivalent of shrooms that's responsible, but it's something else, something about him and about me though, too, feeling not so much like the me I've been recently.

Kurt picks up my mug and walks ahead of me toward the bedroom. He pauses by the doorway, gesturing for me to go through. "The towel warmer's on, and I've been leaving that light..."

I watch him point out a couple other things that have

been here since the late Paleolithic period.

He gestures to the living room. "I'll be there."

I offer to sleep on the couch, but he shakes his head.

"No, I'm good there," he says. "It's more comfortable than it looks. I slept on it my first night on the mountain."

I run my fingers over a soft blue blanket that's folded over the foot of the bed. "You were sharing the cabin?" I realize I've said this out loud. "Not that it's any of my business," I add quickly. "Sorry. That's a personal question." I refold the blanket, for no reason in particular, into a triangle.

"No, it's not." He shakes his head and kind of laughs, but uncomfortably, like Huntley watching *Seinfeld* after too many bananas. "And no, I wasn't sharing the place. I was just up late working that first night, and I guess I fell asleep out there."

"Consulting stuff," I clarify.

"Consulting stuff," he confirms.

I look at the sleigh bed, where the tusks of a dead boar are centered over the headboard. "It wasn't the boar?" Of course it was the boar. The boar drives everyone out. It's almost as bad as my last date's swordfish, but I try to think of it as more of a Gliel eccentricity than as an innate character flaw.

"Is that...it's a boar?" Kurt asks. "Like a tusked pig?"

And I know we're drunk on something real, because

we're both laughing when he snorts. Or maybe I snorted. It was probably me.

I briefly explain the history of the boar and admit I've begged Gliel to take it down since it first moved here when I was eleven.

Kurt inquires if it's been rotting these several years, which I also suspect, and I tell him he's been given Gliel's favorite cabin; he reserves the one with Andrew—that's the boar, named after his son—for the people he *likes*.

Kurt grins. "So, the couch...it might have been a little bit because of Andrew, that first night."

"So giving me your bed..." I feel a hiccup emerging at the "his bed" part. I drive off an icy embankment, and hours later, I'm sleeping in this man's bed. My karma must be pretty great. "It's not actually a chivalrous thing at all."

"Of course not." His eyebrows twitch as he smiles.

"You're worried about Andrew giving you nightmares."

"Or falling and stabbing me with a tusk," he admits. "But I know *you're* not scared of a little boar, because you thought I was a...was it a yeti?"

I laugh. And definitely snort this time.

"...a yeti, and you got out of the car anyway. So I'm sure you're gonna sleep fine with Andrew there."

I watch as Kurt flips on the bathroom nightlight.

"It was really nice to talk a stranger tonight," he says.

I turn back to refolding the blanket, muttering something in agreement, and wish him a good night.

I sit up for a while watching the snow, my heart still racing from cocoa and whatever else changed in me over the last hours. When I finally climb into the big sleigh bed, I'm sure, whatever's going wrong with the rest of the mountain, that some of my good karma has finally turned up.

6

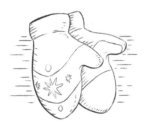

My karma doesn't keep through the next morning, and I get back to town with jumpy nerves and a knot on my head, craving cocoa. My house feels too cold when I finally get home with the truck I borrowed from Adam, and then Faye isn't expecting me to drop by her shop. At least not in one piece.

"It was like there was an explosion." Faye stirs her cappuccino into a little caffeinated cyclone as she takes a seat on her favorite orange pouf. "Like a gas leak, only...bigger. Those cabins still have gas stoves, don't they?"

"Uh huh."

She leans over the table, preparing to melt into a puddle of witch. "I don't get it. Seriously, I..." She pauses, rolling her eyes. Recently, Faye hasn't been able to take herself seriously.

People used to come from all over the country to have Faye read their palms, their tarot cards, and their minds. All that was even more impressive before I redecorated her shop to be more psychic-vibey, though Faye's kept a Noble Roman's tiffany lamp over her reading table in spite of my frequent protests.

For years, though, even pizza chain energy couldn't stop her. Faye's predictions, like those of her great-aunt Beatrice, were eerily accurate even when not particularly welcome; she foresaw everything from unplanned pregnancies to names to go with DNA testing strangers' kids.

Then, about a year ago, Faye foresaw a beloved local Christmas tree farm, Harker's, would be wildly successful. She encouraged them to invest in more tree-growing land because something in her gut told her it would pay them back big time.

But that particular time, it seems the something she felt in her gut was an imbalance of intestinal flora, as Lauren diagnosed it, and not her gift. Three months later, Harker's announced it was starting the process of filing for bankruptcy. Later that evening, Faye started making cappuccinos and stopped doing readings for good. Then she chopped off her hair.

And then, last night, a vision of an explosion in the cabin invaded her recurring dream about a dog, with no tarot cards, no palms, and not even my head here to examine. I'd tell her I've been daydreaming about a yeti, if it would make her feel better, but I don't really think it would.

"Something might have happened after I left," I offer. I don't *know* there wasn't a gas leak, after all, and I was definitely feeling the effects of something that seemed pretty hallucinogenic in the cabin. When I woke up this morning, I convinced myself it was just a feeling brought on by a minor concussion and the trauma of the wreck.

Faye shakes her head. "I haven't seen anything like it in a long time," she says. "I saw you in the cabin, and there was just..." She waves her arms around like a crazy psychic woman you'd expect to find on a mountain like ours. "There was so much energy around you. Popping. Sparking. *Exploding.*"

When I don't offer up any explosions from last night, she stands and goes back to her cappuccino maker, pumping furiously at something on its side. I've never thought of Faye as a violent person; she's all about reading and using energy, and she sells bonsai trees and other good feng shui cures here in the store. But then, I'm supposed to be all about reading and using energy in my job, too, and it took all my willpower not to smother a lawyer with a throw pillow yesterday. But that was just because there was so much beige and he was such an asshole.

"You know, it might have been one of the other cabins," I offer when Faye comes back to her pouf. But I can tell by the way she's gulping her still-steaming cappuccino that she's convinced she's wrong, for the second time now in less than a year, and that this indicates she's a verifiable non-psychic.

"The energy was around *you*," she says, "and you just found a cabin and went to sleep."

I gave her a somewhat abbreviated version of last night. "I had a wreck first," I remind her. "And I had a headache, from the whiplash."

She shakes her head. "It wasn't a crashing kind of explosion."

I've never really gotten how Faye sees things. To me, exploding energy would be like if you mixed reds and oranges and added a little lime green in, say, a bathroom tile. But the kind of energy Faye reads doesn't come color-coded.

I gulp down the last sip of her Amazon-bought hot cocoa, which tastes nothing like Kurt's—Kurt, who I'm trying not to think about today.

When Faye asks for more detail regarding what potentially explosive adjectives might have occupied my thoughts in the cabin, I tell her about the meeting in Roanoke, instead. Because violent explosions seem more likely to be the result of beige-officed lawyers than yeti attraction. And also because there's no good way to tell a small, nosy village you just spent the night with a stranger in the forest. An attractive stranger, no less, who was briefly dressed from the waist up like a yeti.

Faye's frowning as I get up to go, and I wonder if she can read my mind.

"It's going to be okay," she tells me, like I'm the one praying for respite from a dog dream. She keeps saying that, about orange foam and everything else Heslein, too.

"Sure." I force a smile, because no one wants a sad psychic on their mountain around Christmastime.

"Really," she says, handing me a recycled to-go mug on my way out the door. "Take another cocoa. It'll all work out soon."

7

The next day, I wake up thinking of yeti and don't turn on my phone until I'm finishing my lunch at the inn. It lights up with a chorus of beeps, all of them city council-related, and I don't know why I'm disappointed. I didn't give Kurt my phone number, and there wasn't any reason to think he'd try to track me down to return any snowlogged Snickers I'd left behind or anything.

"So it would be good to call soon, but it's not an emergency." Jane's voicemail sounds suspiciously like the woman who reads "To speak to a representative, press…"

"It's not especially helpful news," she clarifies. "But it's not hopeless."

I'd stop by her place on the way home, but I'm not in the right mental space to face Jane's textureless charcoal walls. Last year, she called me over before a bridge tournament because she thought she had a turquoise emergency. That's what she called it, a turquoise emergency. It turned out to be a gift from her mother, a set of silk throw pillows that were almost blue. Almost. They still looked pretty gray to me. It was her turn to host the Piney Falls bridge club—seven octogenarians and her—and she thought the pillows might be too much on the settee, they were so startling to her gray sensibilities.

But Jane works hard to be optimistic and welcoming as a city council member, and I know by how difficult it sounds for her to say it *isn't* hopeless that it is. Eventually, we'll have to acknowledge all the good chi in the world won't airdrop us the millions it would take to push Heslein out of town legally. We're just buying time now, deluding ourselves and throwing salt over our shoulders and hoping for some kind of Hallmark holiday miracle before they break ground on the factory in the new year.

The wind cuts through my pants as I hurry away from the inn, and the achy cold that usually doesn't seep into my joints until January spreads over my back and shoulders. I try to summon some happy, warm yeti energy as I tighten my scarf.

I think these are called escapist fantasies, and you're supposed to pair them with deep greens and blues, like rooms showcasing exotic locales meant to calm your spirit and transport you to a better emotional state or giant, stargazing skylights meant to inspire romantic dreams.

I've never considered a yeti-themed room before, but I can see it clearly now—a thick cream flokati rug by a curved stone fireplace and a wall of glass facing the woods. A leather sofa. A clawed end table. Kurt.

Then, when I reach the truck I borrowed from Adam just off the square, Kurt himself materializes a handful of yards in front of me. In this light, he looks more like a tall thin mint than a yeti. My stomach growls, and I marvel at my ability to be attracted simultaneously to Bigfoot and girl scout cookies. I should probably let Lauren check my hormones.

I unwind the scarf from around my mouth and flap my mitten in a wave. "You're here," I observe when he reaches me. *Here* being both in a corporeal state and *here*, in town. He mentioned last night that he hadn't made it to town yet.

We make the kind of small talk I guess you do when you spend the night together after a winter vehicular emergency, and I find myself staring at his chest as he tells me how charming he's found downtown Piney Falls. I nod vacantly at his torso, imagining the yeti coat there. I might have developed some kind of trauma-induced kink.

He says he was just at the post office and compliments our streetlamp wreaths.

I follow his eyes to the topiaries in front of town hall. I tried to tell the landscaping committee a giant *P* in the middle of the square was a bad idea—largely because it's top heavy, resting at a 45 degree angle that makes it look like cheap abstract art—but I was away visiting Lauren for the crucial unanimous vote and outweighed by an outpouring of community spirit. Since we're the only town on the mountain, we have kind of a surplus of that.

"You saw the landscaping?" I ask. There's an *A* right next to the leaning *P*. We couldn't neglect either Piney Falls or the Awe Wilderness Refuge, since we're the only town near the preserve and not including the Native American name for our river seemed wrong. So the only real landscaping on the mountain features the postal abbreviation for Pennsylvania.

The topiary letters are flanked on either side by small trees decked out in red, green, and blue bows. Sometimes, I think my being born here was the universe's idea of a practical joke.

Kurt nods, smiling. "Do you work near here?" he asks.

I try to focus on our conversation rather than on his chest and my existential woes.

"I'm sorry," he adds. "Is that a personal question?"

"No," I tell him. "I'm an interior designer."

He grins, and I flush. I probably really do need some blood work. It's like twenty degrees out here.

"I had an idea it was something like that, actually," he says.

"You did?" Did he Google me? Did Gliel tell him? So many perilous questions intrude normal waking hours after you spend the night in a stranger's bed. Lauren should have warned me about these.

"I noticed you made the bed with different pillows," he offers.

I look at my boots, but I can't help but be impressed he noticed. Maybe I should be spending more time with men who don't have swordfish or wild boar nailed to their walls.

"And, you, uh....you switched around the paintings in the bathroom."

"Oh."

He nods at the bowl I picked up for Annie. "So, you have a bowl for those candy bars now?"

"I was just delivering them. We have a new vet moving in on the square."

"And you're taking her candy? That's nice."

"I usually take cookies," I brag. "I bake." I can preheat the oven, anyway, and cut the dough into half inch slices from the little cylinder. "But I had the extra candy bars."

"The ones from the binder," Kurt clarifies.

"Right." My makeshift self-defense binder, which hopefully I didn't identify this way. "And, you know, another round of girl scout cookies will be coming before long, so she'll be overwhelmed with thin mints."

We discuss the merits of various girl scout cookie varieties, and Kurt mentions he has an addiction to a new kind with dehydrated mushrooms. I think I'd hold this strangely healthy preference against him if I could, and that I could if just looking at him didn't make me think of fireplaces and soft sweatpants and hot, heavenly cocoa.

Faye's great-aunt Beatrice passes by the parking lot on her way to lunchtime gossip at the inn, and I'm relieved she's too bundled up to see us. Usually, she can detect strangers several yards away, and everyone knows that if you share an attraction with Beatrice, there's some otherworldly force that compels her to throw in a free, but remarkably accurate foretelling of the heartbreak to befall you. Also, selfishly, I don't think I'm ready to share my concussive after-effect with the rest of the mountain yet.

"But I haven't been to the inn," Kurt's saying.

"The inn?"

"You said it was the best place to eat on the mountain."

This is the problem with escapist fantasies; they interfere with focus. "Right." Of course I did; the inn's the *only* place to eat on the mountain.

"Or John said there's a little sushi place on the other side of the refuge. In Radford, I think?"

"John?"

"Your mayor. John Gliel?"

"Right. There is."

Kurt frowns. "You don't still have a headache, do you?" he asks.

I shake my head, feeling dizzy. Kurt blurs a little. Which makes him look even more like a thin mint.

"Would you want to get dinner?" he asks, possibly not

for the first time.

"Oh!" *Oh.* "Yes. Of course." *Of course,* my shake-addled brain echoes.

Kurt's eyes meet mine, and heat creeps up my neck. "And maybe we could ask each other personal questions," he says.

I feel my face contract in a smile.

"Tomorrow?" he asks.

I nod.

"And sushi? Instead of the inn?"

I nod again. "Sushi," I echo as we walk towards Adam's truck.

"Is six okay? And it's okay if I pick you up?"

I rummage through my bag for the keys, smushing a couple interiors magazines. "Great," I tell him.

Kurt watches me for a minute as I pull out the keys. "You'll get in a car with me," he confirms, "voluntarily."

"Of course."

He grins. "Even though I'm a stranger."

"No one's a stranger in Piney Falls," I repeat, grateful my work on the council has finally come to something. Our town motto's printed right on the plaque under the leaning *PA.*

Kurt laughs, and I give him directions to my house, or at least stand there for a minute and make jabbing motions up the hill with the keys.

"Great," he says.

I stop gesturing and extend my hand.

He shakes the offered mitten. He's not wearing mittens.

"I'm happy I ran into you," he says.

I mumble something I hope is reasonably coherent, but he's smiling, and I'm overheating. He had me even before sushi.

8

One major downside to escapist fantasies is that they're prone to interruption. The next day, my lunch goes cold as my home is invaded by my fellow city council members.

"A sports complex," I echo. Lucy Lowens wants to use the money we were counting on to cover our suit against Heslein for a *sports complex*. "And you're sure?" I ask, wobbling on the edge of my sofa as I grip a throw pillow in my lap. I knew I shouldn't have done my living room in dark reds. Yellow would have been so much more cheerful.

"I'm afraid so," Jane says, picking at her fingernails. I think she got this from Gliel.

"And you know because..."

"She called me." Jeff says 'called' like a phone call was out of line to begin with.

I swallow a gulp of tepid coffee.

"She thinks her grandson's going to be a soccer player," Jane offers. "Anyway, I thought you should know before she…"

Jeff stands and starts pacing, and Jane's voice trails off. Since he's been back on the mountain, I've been worried about Jeff wearing out the original hardwoods at his grandparents' old cabin. Jeff definitely belongs on concrete.

"She wants me to build a *mudroom*."

"A changing area," Jane corrects. Jane's our resident writer and can make anything sound better.

"And she doesn't even want solar panels."

"Solar panels," I echo, clutching the throw pillow a little tighter to my stomach.

"She wants a soccer field," Jane adds. "There's enough land for…"

"She thought the panels would *detract*, that's what she said. From how it looked. The mudroom," Jeff repeats. "She wants me to build a *mudroom*."

Jane reaches out to touch his arm, then evidently thinks better of it. "But she's wanting to be, uh…local about the harvesting," she says. "She told Jeff that she wants the bleachers to be naturally finished hardwood." Jane looks at me expectantly, I think actually expecting some design critique of naturally finished hardwood bleachers.

"Hardwood," I echo, because this is about all I can manage right now.

"So I think it's time..." Jane goes back to picking at her nails. "I mean, I think we should release some kind of a statement. Maybe in the newsletter, before she says anything in public, that..."

"It's over," Jeff finishes for her.

Jane wrinkles her nose. "We could say that better," she says.

"That we're broke," I offer. That the hotshot lawyer Heslein hired to stop us really has, and that there's no way to put off them turning our mountain into an uninhabitable smog pit burbling with orange foam, new sports complex for Lucy Lowens' grandson or not. "That the lawsuit's hopeless."

"That our legal fees are unsecured," Jane says.

"But the lawsuit, if we can't pay our..."

"It's over," Jeff repeats.

Jane's nose twitches.

I turn away and focus on my breathing. I try to summon all the blue energy I can, try to forget I'm in the middle of a blood red living room—maybe not my best decision—when our mountain's about to lose all its evergreen areas and replace them with gray factory buildings and foamy swampland.

I manage to keep my voice in the range of those cool,

soothing tones as we cover the need to give everyone in Piney Falls a heads up. The surrounding land owners will need to know so they can negotiate the best prices together, and a few young couples who are trying to get pregnant will need to go somewhere else, and everyone with kids will want to know about the asthma rates and the projected deaths even a population as small as ours will suffer from the particulate matter from the smokestacks.

I try not to sound too panicked when I leave a message on Gliel's answering machine. It's the first time I can remember that he hasn't answered his phone.

Afterwards, Jane, Jeff, and I agree to keep this between us for now. Everyone else will be at the inn to celebrate Adam's birthday tonight, and the lawsuit news would only ruin their good mood. I make plans to work on the press release with Jane first thing in the morning. But when she and Jeff leave, the reds get me.

9

It's around ten till five when Kurt pulls up in a rented silver SUV, interrupting my extended fantasy about running down Heslein's lawyer with a snowmobile and forging Lucy Lowens' name on a big, fat check to the council before chucking her over the waterfall.

I'm pretty sure it started with mantras of acceptance. I left the reds of my living room to surround myself with the soothing greens of the woods beyond my porch, bundled up like a giant, peace-loving cheesecake in my soft cream puff coat. I tried telling myself it'll all be okay when Heslein invades; energy can't be created or destroyed, and so all the good energy on Piney Mountain will radiate out with its inhabitants as many of us move on, spreading goodness all over Appalachia and beyond.

I told myself that. And then I went right back to

daydreams of murdering the lawyerly and elderly.

I pull open the door of Kurt's SUV and climb into the seat before he can get out.

His forehead contracts as he reaches for a watch under a couple layers on his wrist. "I'm late?" he asks. "Is mountain time..."

"You're early."

He looks back at me. When I meet his eyes, my murderous rage fades at least a little.

"I wanted to wait outside," I tell him as I unzip my coat. You'd think an interior designer could live in her own interior space a little more comfortably.

"I was worried I might have taken the wrong road," Kurt says. "My phone lost reception when I got halfway up the..."

I hit my forehead on an air vent as I jerk an arm out of my coat sleeve.

"Are you all right?"

Heat courses around the right side of my head and pulses between my now almost-visible-to-passerbys crash bump and where the other side of my forehead's just collided with the air vent. If this one swells, too, I'll have little horns like Darth Maul.

"Fine," I manage. "Did you have GPS?" I lay the puff coat across my lap and turn to face Kurt.

He's already facing me. I'm already overheating. I wonder if this is what dating feels like for Lauren. Maybe she's so glowy because she sweats so much.

"Your head," he prompts.

"It's nothing," I say, taking couple of the yoga fire breaths Lauren taught me. My forehead pulses in time. *Ser-en-i-ty, Ser-en-i-ty...*

"I got your street address from the phone book," Kurt offers. But his hand's still on the gear shift. "I found one in the town hall. From 1997."

I tell him about the great Piney Falls census-taking of 1997, when we cataloged all the mountain's residents and their relatives who'd moved away, from cousins fanning out through the Virginia area to Beatrice's brother, who's believed to have gone to Mars. They're labeled under each resident's name "cousin in New York," "sister," "ex-wife," etc.

As I get to the origin of the initial ex-wife included in the book, Kurt leans towards me, and I stop talking. His hand settles at my forehead. It twinges as he pushes back my hair.

"Have you had this looked at?" he asks. "From the crash?"

"It's going down," I lie. But my voice comes out shaky. "You're...you're not a doctor, are you?" In my head, Kurt's remained a photography consultant, using the term in a sexy, artistic way. I hope he's not here to consult on Lucy Lowens' gout or something.

He promises he's not, and then small talk occupies us on the drive into Radford. The wind's picking up, and red-ribboned wreaths blow around on the lampposts as we get closer to town. Radford's the nearest semi-anonymous place you can go without straying too far from the mountain, the kind of place you can sit outside on cafe patios during the summertime and drive through the neighborhoods to see the lights around Christmas without being stopped by anyone you know.

We park on a side street just outside the town square and walk to the sushi restaurant tucked into a corner. The wind down here's lighter, a breeze that doesn't make it through my outer layers. It makes me feel like I've stepped into a different world tonight, maybe even into a different person.

As Kurt and I drink our first glasses of an effervescent red wine, we cover everything from roadway salt corrosion to the dangers of harsh overhead lighting. The meal goes quickly, easily. Not like I haven't been on a dinner date in years or like I almost attacked this man with a binder full of chocolate bars just a couple nights ago. I guess Kurt gets out more often than I do.

At some point, I glance over and realize a pianist has started playing Christmas music on the baby grand in the corner of the restaurant. There's something about the way time passes with Kurt, the way this hour's gone by without being felt. We scan the dessert menu, deciding to split a specialty cheesecake I imagine is just the color of a yeti.

"You haven't told me about the thing you were

working on in Roanoke the night of the wreck," he reminds me when we're midway through the cake and have been quiet for a minute, as though something so sweet and decadent had be tempered by orange factory foam.

As I push around some raspberry sauce with my spoon, I remind myself have a duty not to burden an out-of-towner with Heslein business. Up until this point, my most unpleasant thought since Kurt picked me up has been about the possibility of my avocado roll giving me sesame breath.

"I want to know. Really," he says, and there's something so sincere about my yeti when I meet his eyes that makes me want to tell him everything.

So I don't hold back any of the gritty details as I tell him about Heslein, and about the town Bakeoff that Beatrice wins every year, and the blue ribbon-tying ceremonies every spring on the lampposts to honor the wooly bears, when the town has strawberry daiquiris to celebrate coming out of hibernation, and about all the other reasons this community and the preserve really are worth preserving.

And the way he's listening, the way he's sitting quietly watching me from across the table, makes me feel like I'm not a babbling idiot holding a "Save PA" banner and getting ready to chain myself to a waterfall.

"You'll think I'm crazy," I finish weakly after dipping

into a long rant about particulate pollution estimates and orange foam.

Kurt smiles, and for a second, I have that sweet, tingly sensation of burying my toes in a thick flokati rug.

"I don't," he says. "I think you love your town. I wish I had a home like that."

As he tells me about his childhood, he doesn't seem to notice my scraping away at the last of the cheesecake's chocolate crust. Kurt was born outside Phoenix, AZ, and a combination of education, fate, and what I can only assume is my own excellent karma brought him to our mountain.

I'm trying to decide on my next personal question to ask him when he asks if I'd like to dance, instead. He gestures to the pianist, who's just transitioned into a slow "Christmas Song" as a few couples sway over by the kitchens.

I nod, finally out of words. Kurt takes my hand as we walk to the dance floor, and my feet somehow step into place like there aren't a dozen raised floorboards to trip over. His hand resting at the small of my back makes me forget about the pain in my head, too, and about all the other pains, months of repressed Heslein hostilities and baby blue ballrooms.

My hand finds his shoulder, and I rest my fingers on the soft wool of his sweater. He smells like peppermint Zum bar, and I feel like I've been this way, leaning into him, so many times before. Not like we just met the day before yesterday. And definitely not like I mistook him for a yeti and almost assaulted him with a binder full of chocolate bars.

I stay unseasonably warm the rest of the dance and the entire drive back to up the mountain. I shouldn't have worn cashmere tonight, I think, even in a cool green.

The twinkle lights illuminating front lawns as we climb the back road remind me it's almost Christmas, and we talk about Christmas mornings and leftover honey-baked ham and overdone trees until we hit the gravel of my driveway.

Kurt puts the SUV in park and is around the hood to walk me in before I think to open my door and step down into the snow. He's saying something about the town when we pause on my front porch.

"I hope it all settles in your favor," he says.

It takes me a second to understand, and I realize I haven't thought about Heslein for a while. I thank him for listening, though I'd hoped he'd forgotten at least some of my save-the-mountain spiel.

His face is a silhouette against the porch light. "Maybe we could go back to town next week and drive through the lights," he says. "I'll be away for a few days, but I was hoping…I'd like it if we could do this again."

I nod, feeling like a piñata full of glitter has burst inside my brain. He takes a step back and looks at me.

Maybe I made a noise. Maybe the piñata did.

"Is that hurting?" he asks. His voice is soft, an echo that bounces between my head-bumps.

I realize I've inadvertently lifted a hand to the newest, still invisible one, which could possibly be receiving some sort of alien signals. Or maybe this is just something about Kurt and his body so close to mine, my trauma-induced yeti fantasy come to life. I turn, getting ready to assure him my head's okay, except for that bursting feeling, but he's stepped in front of me.

And I know I should be asking so many questions right now. *How many plane rides away is California? Are you sure you don't have a wife? Do you own any variety of stuffed fish?* But I can't seem to form any of them.

My body's buzzing with an energy that hits me even harder than the crash did. It's like wading through a sea of tiny sparks or that quiet, ethereal shimmer behind my eyelids right before I passed out at the wooly bear festival when I was nine years old and had done too much spinning in circles.

The buttons of Kurt's coat brush against mine, and I swear I can feel warmth through all the layers between us. In the briefest moment his lips touch mine, I don't care if his home is furnished to resemble to the inside of a whale, complete with seal fat and rotting teeth.

My face is on fire when he steps back and asks again

if I'm all right. The energy's pulsing around us now, and it feels like there were just a thousand explosions inside my skull, but I respond, I hope, with something more reassuring.

We say good night, and I watch him drive away from my living room window. Later, I think I'll say that I understood all this, that this was part of my plan all along. And the universe's. I knew my good karma would catch up with me eventually.

10

The next morning ushers in one of those rare sunny days in the middle of a frigid mountain winter. My old wooden floorboards glisten as I skate over them in my socks, and the sunlight shoots a shiny, happy energy into even the darkest corners of my living room.

After a quick bowl of the new organic chocolate cereal I got at the general store on a whim last week, I dig through my closet for some Christmas candles and arrange them on the mantle between my skating snowmen. But I'm thinking of Kurt again—by the tree, in the pew beside me at the pageant, at the stove making cocoa on Christmas eve. It's the sunshine. Its energy's unstoppable.

My computer makes a cheerful *whoosh* as it powers up. Google shows dancing reindeer above the search bar today, and it's like the whole world's gleeful, having tilted the wrong way on its axis to bring us a little bit of spring before we're plunged into the longest dark of winter.

I'm only a little surprised not to have an email from Gliel in my inbox; if ever there were a morning for forgoing office work and holding a town rally, it would be today. Piney Falls has a reputation for outdoor rallies on warm winter days, town-designated holidays, and anytime we find a woolly bear over 75% brown.

I watch the reindeer on my home screen dance for a minute before plugging in my Christmas tree and slipping into some yoga pants to go join in the sunny weather festivities.

Adam's truck starts with a groan, and I count the window trees as I drive into town. Next weekend, we'll be in full porch-lighting mode, then roof-lighting, complete with sleighs, the week of Christmas.

As I think about the lighting season, I lose some of the morning's shiny feeling. Visitors almost never stay through the holidays. And there are already reindeer on the Google homepage, so I know it's only a matter of time before Kurt returns to the consistent sunshine of Los Angeles and hot cocoa with his own family.

I think I must just be imagining some clouds have rolled in over the mountain when I step down from the truck and knock on Gliel's front door.

The lights are off inside, so I pick my way around the

bushes to his living room window. His Christmas tree isn't on. I double check the date on my cell phone. It's two Tuesdays before tree lighting, three until the pageant and the Bakeoff. Faye's been worried our longtime mayor's mind has been slipping lately, but I've never known Gliel to miss a lighting. He must have gotten overexcited about the prospect of a fair weather rally in December and forgotten to check his calendar.

I try his cell phone again, but there's no answer. My stomach drops when his door handle doesn't turn. We never lock our doors in Piney Falls; our open door policy is on a plaque by the town hall. My head twinges as I fish out a spare key from under the ceramic frog on his front step.

Inside, I don't find a body or anything smelly—maybe I really was expecting the worst—but Gliel's computer is unplugged. I lock the door on my way out and think I hear thunder as I hurry back to Adam's truck and drive the rest of the way into town.

When I get to the square, it looks like the community in pretty much its entirety has gathered in the middle of Main street, but I don't see blue flags or hear music. I have to park on a side street due to all the people, and a blast of cooler air nearly knocks me over when I step down from the truck. No wonder they've ditched the flags; the weather seems to have gone from fair and sunny to full-blown *Wizard of Oz* in about twenty minutes.

Beatrice, wrapped in her usual layers of scarves, is at

the center of it all waving her arms around. I try to sidestep the would-be rally, but the crowd's too thick. And angry. Which isn't a normal reaction to some surprise December sunshine.

"Gone," Beatrice is saying. "I'm telling you, he's *gone*."

I push through a couple teenagers to get to Faye, who's huddled against the front door of her shop and looking very green. And not a festive kind of green. Like fully Elphaba.

"Gliel," she tells me, but then she rushes into her store before I can respond. She waves a hand in front of her face apologetically but looks even more green through the glass of her front window.

"I'm telling you, he's not gone *enough!*" Beatrice shouts. The crowd roars, and she catches my eye, waving me over with the papers in her hand. I step around some of the Martins' grandkids.

"He's in Florida," she says as soon as I get to her, handing me the paper. "I felt it first thing this morning. He's gone, and he's not coming back. At least he'd better not."

I look up at Beatrice, the best psychic Virginia has ever known and the last woman on Earth or beyond you'd want to piss off within three weeks of the Piney Mountain Bakeoff, and feel a very real kind of fear myself.

She's radiating red. The paper's a deed for the final bit of land Heslein needed to get started building the factory. It has John Gliel's name on it, with a transfer order to

Heslein, LLC.

The freezing rain starts before the mob can deliver the paper to the inn's fireplace and ride their snow shovels to Florida in pursuit of our traitorous mayor.

11

By dinnertime, there's a slippery coat of ice that makes everything it touches look like marble, and the only place with power is Adam's pub, which can run for a while on its generator. The Piney Falls townsfolk couldn't drive their cars or even fly on their shovels to aid in the annihilation of our now ousted mayor in Florida, so the best we can hope for is that the karma gods have left him stranded in some swamp infested with a bunch of resentful ex-pet pythons.

Piney Mountain is radiating an aura of vengeance. To make matters worse, Adam's just announced he's running low on sticky bun dough. And everyone knows you can't feed an angry mountain in an ice storm when you're dealing with a sticky bun shortage. Beatrice declared a state of emergency over an hour ago.

Jeff, who's been pacing between the kitchens and the front of the inn for the last twenty minutes, looks especially affected.

"Have you seen Faye?" he demands when he finally pauses by the booth I'm sharing with Jane.

"Faye?" I ask.

"Can't find her. She's not in her store."

I glance around the inn. The town's been gradually trickling in since the sleet started, but there's no Faye in sight.

"Have you thought something might be up with her store?"

"Up with her store?" I ask.

Jeff's eyes are wide and white, a little like I imagine a wendigo's would be. "Yeah," he says. "You know."

I shake my head. I *don't* know. Other than the Noble Roman's lamp she refuses to get rid of and that ugly espresso machine that hails back to the 80's and sounds like a Boeing 727, I haven't noticed any particular issues with Faye's store.

"He thinks it's haunted," Jane offers. "I told him there was a violent death at that address. You remember the article, don't you, about Beatrice's grandma finding a dead girl? I've got it here somewhere." She turns back to her netbook and begins searching through her text documents. Jane's way of responding to the state of emergency was to curl up with her laptop and two extra external batteries.

"That's not what I mean," Jeff says. But his face says that's exactly what he means.

I offer to go back to Faye's store to give it a second look, because there are only so many places you can hide on the mountain in the middle of an ice storm, and I leave as Jeff's pacing by the kitchens and Jane's typing what I'm sure will be an excellent headline about power outages for the town newsletter. Of course, if it were left to popular vote, the headline would probably be about the sticky bun shortage.

Skating across the sidewalk in my tennis shoes is actually pretty efficient, and I'm relieved to at least find the front door of Faye's shop unlocked. I don't know what I was expecting—maybe I was leaning towards something like the Croatia episode from *Supernatural* on the way over. At least we're only two residents down so far.

But Faye's store's taken on an otherworldly feel in a bad way, less *Casper the Friendly Ghost* and more *The Haunting* without the pink bulbs in the chandelier over her coffee counter. I even miss the warm glow of her Noble Roman's lamp. My shoes squeak on the hardwood as I make my way around some tables with the help of my iphone's flashlight.

"Faye? Are you..." Cold air brushes against my legs, and I jump up on a chair and shine the light at the ground. At a very plain and inoffensive burgundy rug.

I hear rustling in the back room and suddenly wish I

had my Snickers binder for protection.

"Lisa?"

I weave around some garden gnomes—stationary, thank goodness, and not even remotely lifelike even in the shadows of the flashlight—and into Faye's reading room. The lace tablecloth billows out toward my ankles, then falls back into place.

"Faye, are you...under the table?"

There's a pause. The tablecloth moves again.

I lift the edge of the cloth and can't for the life of me explain why I feel dread. Maybe it's for my own mental health. They say you're the compilation of your five closest friends, and four of mine live on this mountain.

Under the table, Faye's rummaging through the wooden chest she usually uses as a footrest.

I ask as casually as possible what she's working on, whether she knows there's a power outage, and why she's hiding under a table, but I guess it doesn't come across right.

"Of course I know," she says. Then she scoots back and looks at me like *I'm* the one hiding under a table. "And I'm not hiding," she says. "It doesn't get very cold in here. We're over the main sewer line."

I decide to ignore this from a feng shui standpoint, seeing as we're in a state of emergency. "Jeff's looking for you," I tell her.

Faye's head collides with the edge of the table.

"He was worried. He came to look for you, but..."

"I must have missed him," she says. "I was just getting coffee ready for Adam."

"Coffee," I echo. There's an ice storm and a mass power outage, and Faye goes for the coffee before the shelter. Maybe there really is an issue with the radiation from her microwave. Lauren told her she needs to stay six feet away from it when it's running, but I don't think she's been listening. I'm also starting to think we emphasized eccentric oranges too much in this room. Like they even work in the dark.

I wait for her, reminding myself there isn't really a ghost in the place, but as Faye's getting the last of her coffees together, cold air blasts my ankles again through my pants, and I can't stop shivering.

She's slow getting bundled into a coat and out the door, but somehow, it seems less cold out on Main Street. We skate along on the ice past the new vet's office, where there's light behind the curtains.

I step back to see through the window. It looks like there are candles lit. "We should check on Annie," I say. "I didn't see her at Adam's." There's more light coming from down the hallway, where the kennel's going to be. "Actually, I've *never* seen her at Adam's."

Faye's facing away, zipping her coat higher over her neck. "I don't think she's very friendly," she says. "Maybe she's avoiding everybody."

I want to offer some defense of our new vet, but I have to acknowledge it does seem like we're attracting a fresh breed of nut to our mountain. Annie looked at me like I'd brought her a pile of gold instead of a bowl of Snickers when I delivered them, but she rushed me out of her office before I could check out the exam rooms or the new surgery suite. I've been waiting to offer to repaint for her until the lawsuit's finished, figuring I can only handle so many pastels in my compromised emotional state.

I persuade Faye to wait at the front while I go around to the kennel door.

I knock a couple times before trying the doorknob, and it opens with a creak. All I can make out is the low light of candles in the hallway.

Then Annie skids around the corner in a floral onesie, nearly running into me as she reaches the door. Kurt comes around the corner just behind her, sans shoes and jacket.

12

Back at the inn, Faye has her face scrunched up in Beatrice-in-bad-lemon-tart-eating mode as we watch Kurt usher Annie inside.

"You didn't meet him," Faye says. "I meant to tell you I had. His name's Boxler."

I stare at the table as the word 'Boxler' somehow arranges itself in my imagination as the same Boxler Heslein hired to countersue us, the same Boxler they flew in from California, the same Boxler I mistook for a yeti and kissed on my front porch.

That's when *serenity* goes right out the window. And I thought I was upset when he was just *Kurt* hiding out in a candle-ensconced kennel with Annie without his shoes or outerwear.

"I didn't like him, either," Jane offers. "You know, I even tried to interview him about the lawsuit. Kind of like a human interest piece, you know, so he could tell his side of the story, and he told me he couldn't comment. Can you believe that? He flat out refused to talk to me. Right by the post office."

"The post office," I echo. He said he was coming from the post office when he met me outside the square and asked me to dinner. *The evil, countersuing Kurt Boxler.*

"I saw him go in, and I asked Angela who he was, and she checked the mailing address label, and said, 'That's funny. He's mailing something to Florida,' and I told her to open it, but she said she couldn't, so we tracked the address, instead, and it was to Heslein's headquarters, so I called Adam and asked if he was staying at the inn, and Adam said no one was staying at the inn but a couple of the Martins' grandkids and a few college students from Hollins here for a skiing trip over their holiday break, and so I asked Angela if Gliel's cabins were open, but she said they weren't, and I said I couldn't believe he'd be staying down in Radford and drove all the way up here just to use our post office."

Jane pauses to take a breath. "So I followed him around the square, and I caught up with him by the shrubbery, and he said he couldn't comment. Can you believe that?"

I push myself up onto my feet as Faye voices her concern about not having seen any visions of an orange foam-defending bastard of a lawyer arriving in town.

The sticky bun I ate earlier threatens to leave me, and when I see Kurt walking towards our table, I understand for the first time how the expression "seeing red" originated.

13

"Lisa? Can you hear me? The door's stuck."

I hear Kurt Boxler's shoulder ram into the freezer door and feel some small measure of satisfaction.

"Lisa?" he asks. "Are you out there?"

It's a shame he wasn't still shoeless and coatless when I led him into the freezer. Not that it was his lack of outwear that prompted this. It was definitely the lawyer-come-here-to-sue-us-for-the-evil-corporation-with-the-help-of-our-corrupt-mayor thing. Or at least it should have been just that.

"Can you open the door from your side?" he asks.

The energy buzzing around me now is sour and dark as it pounds between my head-bumps, demanding blood. It's like Kurt, the crash, the lawsuit, and everything else that's gone wrong in the last six months are all catching up with me at once.

I'm about to remind myself to take a breath, to respond rationally, *serenely*, when instead, I develop a case of such angry verbal diarrhea that I can't completely decipher my own my words as they pour out. Loudly. Town landmarks that would be destroyed, something vague but nonetheless enlightening with respect to my own personal religion about lightning and the karma gods. I think I quote the Environmental Protection Act twice. I can't stop it.

Kurt says a few times—shouts, actually, that he can explain, and I tell him not to bother. Maybe not in those exact words, but I'm pretty sure he understands me.

"And you weren't wearing shoes," I finish.

A cabinet in the hallway falls open, probably with the combined force of him pushing into his side of the freezer and all the angry vibrations I'm giving off, and a coconut for Adam's New Years Eve luau tumbles to the floor.

The freezer's gone quiet.

But apparently I'm not finished. I scoop up the coconut as I curse my way through the particulate pollution estimates and the impact of deforestation on the Awe Wilderness Refuge before I have to stop for air again. My face is wet. The coconut in my hand reminds me of creamy coconut milk hot cocoa, and I want to smash it over Kurt's evil lawyer head.

"Lisa?"

I spin to find Adam behind me. He's flanked by Jeff, who looks fully wendigo now.

"Lisa, is the lawyer...in the freezer?"

Jeff steps around him and reaches out a hand to me. "Don't hurt the coconut, Lisa," he says.

I look at the coconut, then at the door, then back down the hallway. Annie chooses this moment to peek around the corner.

"I understand," Adam adds, the way you talk to someone when you're trying to convince them not to jump off a building or something. But I'm not considering jumping off anything. I just want to pummel a lawyer with a coconut.

"I understand exactly why you're upset," Adam continues.

"Yeah," Jeff adds.

"I'm upset, too," Adam tells me. "But that's a perfectly good coconut, and none of us want the lawyer to contaminate the pizza dough."

14

The second coat of putty-colored paint goes on smoothly, covering the last traces of red and filling my living room with sweet, light gray serenity. The trim's fresh and white and goes with the Victorian fainting couch Beatrice had Adam deliver this morning.

I've known for a while that I needed a living room cleanse, but I had no idea it was so obvious to the rest of the mountain. And I've never needed a fainting couch before.

I scoot my desk back up to the window, replacing my pothos and arranging its leaves over the sill. Whatever's happening outside, which I cut off by switching my cell phone to airplane mode and unplugging my internet router, at least harmony's been restored to my living room. And there's a strong sense of freedom that comes from knowing I can pair the gray and white with whatever I want. Turquoise. Lime. Red. Maybe not red.

I take a seat on the fainting couch and study my creation, letting the zero-VOC paint fumes wash over me. It's that sweet smell of new beginnings, something beautiful and so refreshing about a full living room cleanse that softens even the biggest blows. My toes tangle in the sheepskin rug—my effort at making peace with the fuzzy parts of my life—as I settle in for some good paint-breathing meditation.

It took me two full nights to get out of the sea of red in my head and a day a half more for the ice to thaw. The power switched back on around three that morning, spreading light like a beacon from the heavens and a promise the karma gods won't be sending any more evil lawyers to destroy us.

Even if our financial and legal situations are no better, at least we're one lawyer down. Kurt Boxler fled sometime after Adam let him out of the freezer, probably quickly pursued by townfolk with shovels, and hasn't been seen or heard from since. It would be a beautiful kind of poetic justice, I think, if the lawsuit were stalled because his body isn't discovered until spring, maybe scattered about the mountain in bear poo fertilizing the new saplings. I inhale, exhale, and think of *serenity*.

I'm almost centered when my front door swings open

with a blast of cold air and Jeff stomps in, smashing a plank of wood onto my desk. The plank pushes my pothos sideways against the window.

Jeff has a kind of Herman Munster cuddliness about him on good days, but he's the model for the zombie apocalypse when he's on a mission. He knocks the fainting couch out of the way with a swipe of his arm, presumably now channeling Godzilla, and plunks the wood on the floor.

"So, when I said I needed a new floor..." I start.

He picks up the fainting couch and scratches one of its legs noisily across the wood.

"It wasn't an emergency," I finish weakly. Jeff told me there was some new material he's been working with in Oregon, and I hope this isn't an alternative use for waterlogged Christmas trees or something. When people ask me what my floors are, I don't want to have to say "evergreen."

"Do you have any coffee?" he asks.

I shake my head, then watch as he goes to the kitchen and returns with a glass full of water. Which he then pours onto the wood plank. It beads.

He grins and heads for the door. "I'll be back in a couple hours," he says.

He's out the door, the water puddle still intact, before I can respond.

I've wiped up the water, replaced half the books on the shelves, and rearranged my holiday ice skating bears on the mantle when my front door opens again. Only it's not Jeff this time.

Kurt appears in my wall mirror like the thing behind the heating vent on *Signs*. Only he looks...more hot than translucent, and I hate him for this almost as much as I hate him for selling us out to Heslein. I guess this would be a good time to alert the townsfolk with their snow shovels.

I spin to face him and prepare to do my best verbal shoveling of lawyer shit out of my home. This room is sacred now in its soothing grays and purifying whites, not to be contaminated with anything Heslein, orange foamy or, more importantly, lawerly. I tell him this, maybe with slightly stronger language.

Kurt meets my eyes and doesn't move when I stomp up to him. So much for the sheen of the paint reflecting sunshine into my outlook. I want to skewer my yeti fantasy. I want to skewer the *yeti*. And maybe barbecue him.

But he holds his ground. Then he holds out some papers.

I take them. I want to smash them over his head, but they're papers, not a binder full of chocolate bars or a coconut.

The first page is a deed for the land Heslein owns with

a transfer order to the town of Piney Falls. Kurt reaches out and turns the page.

His voice is soft, far away. "It's Heslein's settlement offer," he says.

My body goes limp, real-life-woman-in-need-of-a-fainting-couch. It's the rush of blood, I think, this feeling of weightlessness that has Kurt blurring into a beautiful black bear in front of me.

I can barely make out the text when I look back at the papers. The list of conditions starts with a no-fault clause, a guarantee for our legal fees to date, and a money order for seven million dollars.

I look up at Kurt, then down again, to count the zeros. There are six. *Seven million dollars.*

The energy—not red this time, but something entirely different and dazzling—zings across my skin as I flip through the last of the papers, confirming Heslein wants to settle. By going away and leaving us with seven million dollars and all the land they own on the mountain.

"It turns out Gliel was taking money from the corporation in exchange for transferring the deed to some land," Kurt tells me. "Which I did *not* know. I'm the good kind of lawyer, I promise."

I snort. Now I'm starting to sound like Lauren's bird. I should be too old to believe in good lawyers, like the tooth fairy and the Easter bunny, except on Piney Mountain.

"A *consultant*, you mean," I say when I finally find my voice.

Kurt's laugh is deep, like Huntley when he's about to regurgitate a banana.

I look up at him. I really might need the fainting couch. "You sold out Heslein," I say. And my yeti fantasy returns in full force, goosebumps prickling over my arms as my toes twist in the flokati fibers of my new rug.

"*Heslein* sold out Heslein," Kurt says. Then he walks around to my side and flips through the packet. His hands are warm when they brush mine, and that bright, buzzing energy seems to engulf both of us now.

"You left to..."

"I left to fix it," he says. "And, you know, for personal safety, so you didn't attack me with a coconut. Then I found out your mayor was taking a bribe from the company to approve the zoning and get them that land. So you're also going to have some cabins." Kurt points to a sheet which indicates Gliel's relinquished his properties along the preserve. "And the condo in Florida that was in Heslein's name. It was going to Gliel, too. It's where he is now."

"And Heslein?" It still comes out like a dirty word, but it seems more like a bug to be removed now than like a character on *Predator*.

Kurt's lip twists up, the first smirk I've seen on him. "They filed for bankruptcy this morning," he says. "It would have been worse for them not to pay you and get sued; the board members could have been personally liable. This was their biggest project, and they were counting on it. And before you ask, I did *not* do the filing for them."

I stumble backwards to brace my hips against the side of the fainting couch. It takes a minute for it all to sink in. That this is over. That my yeti saved the refuge. That Piney Falls is seven million dollars richer. And that Andrew the boar's head can now go straight over the waterfall.

My yeti.

"And, at Annie's..." he starts, "it was just my shoes and coat I'd taken off, by the way. You seemed to think...I mean, I was...consulting on something delicate. Something afraid of my outerwear."

When I look at Kurt this time, I don't see any of the expected beige lawyer bullshit. He's full yeti now, the yeti of my daydreams.

He picks up the thermos he set on the counter and extends it towards me. "To celebrate?" he asks.

I sniff, and hot cocoa steam wafts up over my cheeks. It feels like concussive injuries and enemy-blood-drinking and Christmas all at once.

I wrap an arm around his neck, and his hands settle over my waist, enveloping me in his warmth. When he kisses me, he tastes like melted Dove bar and political ecstasy.

I don't have Faye's gift, and I'm fantasizing about yeti, but I have a feeling this is going to be the best Christmas Piney Mountain's ever seen.

Extra Gifts

Faye

I feel the dog's weight on my legs, smell its wet fur and hear panting. Its breath is warm against my cheek and reeks of bacon.

When it licks my chin, my shop comes back into focus. I scan the room, my eyes landing on a tray of fresh pumpkin muffins, then on the cappuccino boxes stacked on the counter and the twinkle lights draped over the doorway. There is, of course, no dog.

The first few times I had the vision were at night, so I initially dismissed it as a recurrent dream my psych background should have prepared me for. But now the dog's coming almost every day, more clearly each time, and I'm pretty sure it's the hairy harbinger of full-blown kookdom.

My bangs fall into my eyes as I fire up the cappuccino machine and toss a leftover cinnamon bun into the microwave. This is my new haircut and my new normal, a kind of unsettled, out-of-place energy that's clung to me for the last several months just like the dog vision.

I watch the microwave count down, running my hands over my hips, but there's no skirt there to smooth. A few months ago, when I cut my hair and changed my wardrobe, I thought I was ready to grow into some other kind of being, post-psychic, but the growth thing hasn't really been happening for me.

The bell on my front door rings, and Steven, my cardiologist, walks in just as the smell of cinnamon bun is starting to waft out of the microwave. I wonder if he can sense the cholesterol at a distance.

Today, Steven surprises me by asking about my feet, instead.

I busy myself with coffee as I answer him and try to look calm—unbothered, you know, *unpossessed*. Even with all my visions being backwards and now dominated by a dog, my cold feet are what's most outwardly symptomatic. The rest of Piney Mountain blames this on my lack of a suitable bed companion, but Steven's still leaning towards borderline hypothyroidism.

"I've been taking the ginkgo Lisa's sister sent," I tell him, like something like ginkgo might actually be able to fix me. I keep forgetting to ask Lisa if Lauren's seeing someone. She'd be perfect for Steven, but she hasn't been back to the mountain for several years and seems to go in and out of relationships like I go in and out of visions.

Steven confirms I haven't tried the thyroid hormone he prescribed yet, and I assure him the ginkgo's helping. It's helping me avoid swallowing the thyroid hormone, at least, and I feel like acknowledging I can't swallow pills is almost as bad as acknowledging I'm having visions of a dog.

He picks up a box of tea from the counter and turns it over, looking through the ingredients. "Are you drinking a lot of caffeine?" he asks.

"Not really." This is a vicious cycle, what happens when everything goes backwards—I see the mountain thriving, giving off overwhelmingly positive community vibes, but all evidence points to our future community consisting of a group of underpaid workers trying to live in a sea of air pollution and orange foam. I see Harker's expanding, and it's ready to file for bankruptcy. I see a dog, and...I don't even know what the opposite of a dog is. It's like having a radio that only picks up the wrong frequency. And the cure can only be more coffee.

I hand Steven a decaf, and he sips at it as he shares the tribulations of his quest to grow tomatoes in his office. He looks at me expectantly at one point, and I wonder if he actually thinks I might make a prediction about this season's indoor tomato growth. My career makes a slight whooshing sound as it's sucked up by the air vents.

"Have you ever thought about a cat?" he asks after a thorough account of the perils of upside down heirloom tomato planting. "You seem like someone who should have a cat."

He must be thinking of witches. I wonder if Steven thinks I'm a witch. He explains that his mom had a cat who slept on her feet and kept them warm, and I promise him I'll consider this. Because he's my doctor, you know, and because I'd rather not directly address that there's nothing else in my bed to warm my appendages.

Our conversation eventually turns to Annie, the new vet who's just moved in across the street. "Jeff was over there yesterday," Steven tells me. "I think he's been doing some duct work for her or something."

I feel like a great ball of bitchy universe hits me in the stomach as soon as he says Jeff's name. It's how I usually feel before a strong vision, except Jeff Harker's always caused this kind of interference, and it's otherworldly only in its effects.

It was Jeff's reappearance in town that brought on the dog dream, just like it's been Jeff who's brought on everything else disruptive in my life since I was about twelve. It started innocently enough, with a little crush when I was a couple years behind him in school. I couldn't string two words together coherently when he was around and used to turn all kinds of colors anytime his name was mentioned. It was the usual kind of childhood crush, I guess, except that it never went away.

I don't know exactly what it is, what kind of energy Jeff gives off that seems to demand its own orbit and sends mine into a tailspin, but its effects are nothing short of debilitating. It let up for a little while in college, when we were in different states, and then when he was in Oregon afterwards, but I could still feel it. And then, about a year ago, it came back with a vengeance. And then *he* came back.

Jeff was, appropriately, the subject of the first vision I had that didn't come true, the beginning of the end of reason and the start of my cold feet. One Thursday last February over what seemed like a perfectly good roast beef sandwich at the inn, I saw the success of his family's tree farm and encouraged them to buy more land. Eight months later, Jeff had to abandon whatever heroic things he was doing with sustainable materials in Oregon to arrange for the company's dissolution after the new year.

"Don't worry," Steven adds. "I don't think it was anything serious with the duct work. Probably nothing you'd have to worry about over here. And did I tell you he's putting solar panels on my roof?"

I say how great this is, hiding my sweaty fingers and asthmatic symptoms from my cardiologist as I bid him farewell. When he's out the door, cold air blasts my ankles, and I push a box in front of the vent by the cash register.

2

Everyone knows the fastest relief for a supernatural headache is one of Adam's fried bologna sandwiches. My extremities are almost warm as I sit in the pub, and I wonder if there's some other magical meat byproduct out there that might be able to convince my stomach Jeff Harker isn't just down the road.

When Adam comes over with more coffee for me, I promise to deliver some more bags of cappuccino mix from Amazon before the weekend crowd gets in. This seems to be my new gift, using the internet to order products from the great beyond Piney Mountain. Word on gifts of this nature spreads quickly; Adam's taken a liking to instant mixes, and the Piney Falls knitting club's now demanding pashmina.

"Can you get one that tastes like pineapple?" Adam asks. He leans over my booth, straightening a wreath on the wall behind me. "I want something special this year for the luau."

I'm tempted to tell Adam his new year's luau has always been a little excessive on the *special,* but as the mountain's resident Amazon genie, I promise to check on pineapple coffee availability as soon as I get back to my computer.

"Is Jeff still at Amy's?" he asks.

"Annie's," I correct.

Adam's forehead wrinkles. "The new vet's not Amy? I could have sworn he said Amy."

"Annie. And I think I saw his truck there when I left," I say casually, because Adam seems to have no idea Jeff's my own psychic bad roast beef sandwich. In fact, Adam considers my role in the whole Harker's bankruptcy ordeal something of a lucky misunderstanding; the inn's now running on geothermal energy from a composting system and has a backup generator, and he has his best friend back in town until the whole company dissolution thing's settled.

"You've met her?" he asks. "The vet?"

"Not personally," I say. All I really know about our newest resident is that she refused a P.O. Box, which to my knowledge had never been done before in Piney Falls.

I guess she's just another sign of discord on the mountain that I didn't see coming.

Adam slides into the booth across from me, glancing over his shoulder to check on the Messingers, whose kids are gorging on hot cocoa and a big bowl of marshmallows in the far corner booth. "Jeff says she's nice, but she's never out. She hasn't been here at all," Adam says. "And you're sure her name's not Amy?"

I nod and gulp a too-hot sip of coffee.

"He's been spending a lot of time over there." Adam's looking at me now, I guess waiting for some confirmation I share his concern that his buddy might become ensnared by our wily new antisocial vet.

"Oh. Really?" I grab a handful of kettle chips and try to look disinterested. Once Jeff's name comes up, pretty much everything tastes like bad roast beef.

Adam nods. "Is she pretty?"

As I tell him that I only caught a quick glance at Annie somethingorother, DMV, with a scarf over her face, I wonder if she'd seem more or less suspicious to me if she weren't needing so much of Jeff's time on her duct work. Probably less suspicious. Definitely less. But then, she *did* refuse a P.O. Box.

"You haven't, you know, seen anything about her?" Adam asks.

"I've barely even *seen* her." And the most impressive disturbance I've felt from the great beyond for months is the dog; I'm clearly the wrong psychic to consult on a shady new resident.

The bell on the door rattles, and in walks that very psychic. My great-aunt Beatrice is wearing a long fuscia peacoat and has a gold scarf wrapped around her ears. She calls a cheerful hello our way before alighting at Mayor Gliel's table.

Something about her hello tells me she's on a mission, and something about her smile in my direction tells me it's not one I'll like. This might have been how my own gift started; it's possible I wasn't seeing anything at all, just getting good at reading her looks when she was seeing things. When Beatrice sees something, the best course of action is to get out of its way.

Adam rejoins me after delivering some hot lemon water to a tired-looking Gliel and a tea to Beatrice. The two are deep in conversation about something that's making Gliel resemble a wilting houseplant. I told Beatrice a couple weeks ago that I didn't see our mayor making it through another Piney Mountain winter. Not that anyone should take my word for it, though; he's only just turned 60, and I'm not seeing anything else right, either.

Then her voice picks up. "I'm just so sorry," she says. But I can see her face and know immediately that, whatever it is, Aunt Beatrice is anything but sorry. "Adam, honey, the tree lighting's two weeks from Tuesday, isn't it?"

Adam's head shoots up. Our town's holiday tree lighting is prime sticky bun season. "Right," he says. "What's is it?"

Beatrice shrugs her shoulders, looking down and fiddling with her scarf. "It's the worst timing," she says. And I can tell she's positively gleeful. "I've seen I'll be out of town those couple days, and I was just asking the Mayor if he could think of *anyone* who could take over the ceremony on such short notice."

On cue, she looks at me. Adam turns my way, too. And then Gliel. Gliel, who knows my public speaking abilities are at a bare minimum right now. At nil, actually.

"It's your off season, isn't it?" Adam asks eagerly. "Until after the holidays, anyway?"

The stupid bologna sandwich flips in my stomach, and I swear I taste roast beef. It's been my off season for the past nine months, and not intentionally. "I've been thinking of...of redecorating the shop," I tell them. "But maybe I could bring some hot chocolate..."

"Oh, wouldn't that be perfect," Beatrice interrupts. "I'll bring over the choir music first thing tomorrow."

I know there's no arguing with this, no way to reason with Beatrice. So I watch helplessly as she and Gliel settle my MC duties for the event and Adam inquires about the kind of lights we'll use on the tree this year. If possible, he'd like to include something pineapple-themed.

I focus on taking deep breaths and shoving chips into my mouth to absorb the stomach acid as they discuss my co-host, which Gliel quickly declines.

"Jeff could do it," Adam offers. "He has so much experience with...you know, with trees."

"Perfect!" Beatrice exclaims, avoiding my eyes. "Such a good boy. I can't believe I didn't think to call him." She's looking at the ceiling with her trademark *Why didn't I think of that?* look, which I know from years of experience to be the most dangerous of all of Beatrice's looks. Beatrice doesn't just see all; she plans it. She has some pull with the universe in these kinds of things, like the energy goes both ways.

"Well," she says, "that's settled, then. I'll leave you and Jeff to figure out the details." Then, with a promise to bring me the invocation she read last year, she saunters triumphantly from the pub before she's even touched her lunchtime tea.

3

That night, I press the red "play" button on my answering machine, and Jeff's voice fills my loft. With it, his energy bounces off the walls and seeps into the rugs and shimmies along my limbs. It makes me lightheaded and a little nauseated, but not in a good, about-to-have-a-legitimate-vision kind of way. In a uniquely Jeff, lose-my-sandwich kind of way.

"Faye..." It's always worst when he says my name. I turn down the volume. There was some part of me hoping he'd forgotten my name and that my cardiovascular and digestive systems had forgotten him and that we might meet on the street one day and not remember each other at all, and maybe then that we could start over.

"...Couldn't find you," he continues. "Thought we could get together to talk about the tree. Call me."

'Together' does bad things to my upper GI, and I wish for a moment that I had some great witchy power to magic 'together' into working for me and Jeff in a way it never has before. We have a long history of running into each other every few years before the universe sends us hurtling off in different directions again.

I sit back against my throw pillows and try to pick up some indication from the universe about what I should do next, short of actually returning his call or fleeing the mountain and turning off my phone for the duration of the holiday season.

I move an unnecessarily ruffled throw pillow from behind my back, and then it hits me—I'll have Lisa take over my half of the tree lighting duties. Then we'll have the most tasteful community tree anyone's ever seen, and Jeff and I won't have to talk about how we talked too late at the last lighting he attended half a decade ago or about his girlfriend then or about his family business I've singlehandedly tanked.

I unhook my cell phone charger and call, but Lisa's phone goes straight to voicemail. She must still be in the meeting with the lawyer in Roanoke. But this could be a good thing, I tell myself; it means she'll be needing to commandeer a decorating project soon to recalibrate her chi meter or whatever.

I fall back onto my bed with a renewed sense of purpose and arrange an extra blanket over my feet before I fall asleep.

But before I can even close my eyes, my feet start to tingle, and I roll over onto my back and feel shaking. Then *I* start shaking. It's an explosion. I see white hot sparks bursting out like a firework. The woods. Lisa. Gliel's cabin. There are sparks again. And then something hairy in the woods, and Lisa again.

I sit up in bed and take a few shaky breaths as I look out my window. Sleet's sprinkling Main Street, tiny white sparks in the lamplight.

Sparks. I see them again when I close my eyes and feel the energy vibrating all around me.

I call Lisa a second time but hang up when her answering machine kicks on. So now I'm seeing another hairy thing, this one with light fur instead of dark, and powerful, bright sparks. Even Lisa will think I've lost it.

The throw pillow falls off the bed as I flip over. My ankles twinge, and I squeeze my eyes shut and try to sleep.

4

Every once in a great while, the universe gloats, putting us mortals in exactly the right places at exactly the right times for a perfect, fatalistic storm that knocks us on our butts.

And Lisa, she insists, has just thwarted such a moment. Late last night, a great bust of energy from beyond hit me with Lisa and a cabin and an explosion. This morning, she's sitting across from me after having spent a quiet night in one of Gliel's cabins without anything at all popping, sparking, or exploding. Not even a microwave. Not even a pop tart.

"I had a wreck first," she reminds me, "and there was the headache from the whiplash."

But I didn't feel whiplash; I felt an explosion, something big and important the universe popped into place last night. Lisa might be radiating a little more crazy energy than usual, but otherwise, the only difference I can see in her are some dark circles under her eyes.

I get her to repeat her story—a very boring one, in which she found a conveniently unlocked cabin after she ran off the road and slept quietly through the night, like Snow White without the dwarves or the drama.

"It was something with *you*," I tell her. "And not in the car." I get up to refill my cappuccino. "You're sure you didn't feel anything...weird?"

She frowns. "Weird?

"I don't know." I smack the side of the cappuccino machine to shake loose some coffee grounds. "I just...I don't know. It was really powerful, and....it's probably just me. There's something wrong with me. Really wrong, I mean. *Dogs*."

I think again about the fur I saw in Lisa's vision, matted and light, and about how different it was than soft, dark fur in my dog vision. Maybe the fur with Lisa was a wolf. Maybe I was seeing Little Red Riding Hood.

"Still dogs?" Lisa asks.

"I mean dog. Just one."

Nothing happens to her face to indicate knowledge of one dog, much less two. And I'm not sure how long this kind of thing can go on, my navigating explosions in my bedroom and then waking up smelling Beggin Bits, before I start to question my *own* sanity.

Lisa asks what I know about Annie and her new vet

practice across the street as I contemplate the possible implications of dark and light fur in separate visions. Maybe it's some kind of symbol of dueling wolves, like in Native American parables of good overcoming evil. Or visa versa. When I sit back down, my ankles get a cold breeze straight through my jeans.

After a while, Lisa picks up the red bowl she's ready to deliver with some candy bars to Annie—and to Jeff, presumably, whose truck is still there—and I try to reassure her about the Heslein situation as I pass her a to-go cup of hot chocolate. She's like an energetic disco ball at a middle school dance, so I assume coffee's out of the question.

When Lisa's gone and I see Jeff walking across the lobby of the vet's office, I hurry away from the window.

*   *

I've restocked a couple shipments of coffees by the time Angela arrives with my new electric blanket, and I find her deep in conversation with Jane in my front lobby.

"It's that lawyer Heslein's brought in," Angela tells me when I reach them. "He came to the post office today, sent a packet right back to company headquarters."

"And he wouldn't give me an interview," Jane adds.

I listen to their complaints, expressing sounds of shared lawyer hatred as I resist the urge to ask whether he's particularly hairy. Maybe I was seeing a rat instead of a dog. Or the fur in my vision could have been a really bad toupee.

Angela eventually hands over my package, having forgotten it in her excitement. It's not very often we have a non-tourist on the mountain, much less a paid ambassador for evil.

As I cut through the tape, I explain my heated blanket hopes for my ankles.

"And this is what Dr. Lowens recommended?" Jane asks.

"Mmm," I say. Technically, Steven's first choice was a very small dose of thyroid hormone, but at least this doesn't involve swallowing any pills.

I pull the blanket out of the box and examine a blue dial that controls the temperature. For a special no EMF blanket—which I thought was important, since it's likely electromagnetic frequencies that are causing my problems begin with—it's relatively unimpressive. The blanket's cream-colored with some light ribbing and a "this side up" label in one corner. I was expecting an obvious kind of magic, but it feels pretty straightforwardly plush.

Jane and Angela pinch around the fabric trying to feel the little wires as I fish out a couple pumpkin muffins for them from under the counter. I take the blanket upstairs once they've reverted to bashing the enemy-lawyer-who-wouldn't-consent-to-an-interview between mouthfulls.

I guess it's a good thing Lisa's missed this lawyer

update. She's usually all about fostering positivity, but her energy's been so off lately, I have a feeling that in the right circumstances, she might be one of those calm, seemingly normal people who just sort of snap one day and go on a mass murdering spree. Or at least a lawyer-murdering spree. Thank goodness we only have the one here.

I sit on the bed and plug in the heated blanket. Heeding the bold print telling me not to sit on it or fold it, I lay it across my feet and ankles and turn the dial to two.

After several seconds, I still don't feel anything, so I ignore the label and fold the fabric around my feet, turning it all the way up to high. My feet start to warm up, and I take a deep breath and lean back into the headboard, closing my eyes and trying to think of anything but dogs or lawyers.

With the newest shipment of coffee unpacked, my afternoon plan's to catch up on rest, drawing the cold out of my body and replacing it with warm, sane energy. I've been meaning to do this for a while, actually—take a bubble bath, enjoy a nap with my lavender heat pack, and sage my loft to cleanse it of whatever funkiness that's been seeping into my consciousness lately. Typical self care, in other words, if you're cursed with a defective psychic receiver and abnormally cold feet.

I spend a few minutes contemplating which bath salts might best draw out the cold as I savor the toasty warmth around my ankles and calves. An SUV chugs by below my window, and I sit forward and peek through the curtains to see if Jeff's truck has left Annie's place yet. It's still there.

A chill sets into my knees then, and I look down instinctively. There's nothing there but a pocket of goosebumps. I run my fingers over my legs and feel a twinge on my thigh—just a spot, like the cold is slowly, inexplicably, crawling up my body. When I stand up, it disappears.

*   *

A couple hours later, I've abandoned my attempt at an afternoon cleansing retreat and am back downstairs when Adam comes by to pick up his latest coffee shipment.

"You must have just missed Jeff," he says. "Jane told him you were here, but he said the door to your apartment was closed and you didn't answer."

I feel a flash of heat over my chest. Heat this time, not cold. Maybe I'm just straight up possessed. "He came here?" I ask.

Adam nods, picking up a pumpkin muffin ready to be thrown out. This one's two days old and hard. The top crumbles when he bites into it.

"About the tree," he says. "He wants to pick out one from the farm."

At least the signals to my stomach are still working.

Adam must not be very sensitive to energetic

disturbances. He reaches into his coat and pulls out his cell phone. "I'll call," he says. "Let him know you're here now."

I shake my head. Little fingers of light trail off the sides of my vision. "I'm going out," I say.

Adam glances down at my pajama pants.

"I was just about to change. I need to...uh...to meet Annie."

"But you'll call Jeff," Adam says, like *this* is the time for me to face Jeff again, when my signals are all messed up and there's an evil, cold-bringing spirit haunting my loft. It's probably the ghost of an angry snowball from the Christmas tree farm.

"About the tree," Adam prompts. "You've got to pick out a tree."

"Oh! I meant to tell him Lisa's taking over for me." And I can't believe I didn't remember this earlier, when Lisa was in the shop telling me about her explosion-free evening.

"Lisa?"

"For the decorating," I say, because Lisa *will* do all the decorating when she hears my thoughts. She just doesn't know it yet. My tree would probably have Noble Romans lamps. "I'm hoping it'll take her mind off Heslein," I add.

Adam nods, pacified, and takes another bite of the crumbling pumpkin muffin.

I indulge his discontent on the lack of appropriately luau-themed coffees available online for a while and help him load a box of something plain and Columbian into his Escape.

As he drives away, I see Jeff's truck's still at Annie's, and I shuffle back inside to face my snowball ghost alone.

5

The next Tuesday, I wake up on my stomach with no dogs in sight and the sun streaming in through my curtains. *Sun*, in December. I feel an unexpected burst of positive energy as soon as I push up onto my elbows, like a great psychic cloud has lifted from over Piney Mountain. My desk glistens. My bedcovers are streaked in sunshine. My butt's cold.

My butt. The snowball demon—and I'm sure now it's a demon, because spirits aren't this persistent—has moved up to my butt. But even a cold butt can't stifle the feeling of brightness that's washed over the mountain this morning. Warmth slowly trickles down my backside as I stand. Other than the snowball demon moving closer to my vital organs, everything seems to be right in my little loft.

Everything, that is, except this nagging reminder in the pit of my stomach that it's Tuesday and that I'm meeting Jeff this afternoon to discuss the tree. Because apparently he thinks the tree needs discussing, and he doesn't want to discuss it with Lisa.

I felt him before I saw him yesterday. I was standing against the counter with my head pulsing, my fingers twitchy, and my stomach full of butterflies—psychic butterflies, you know, like a scene from *The Birds*.

He asked how I was. I told him my pumpkin muffins were burning. Adam, always eager to lend a hand where muffins are involved, delivered them safely from the oven and even managed to scarf down a couple before they'd cooled. Then Jeff asked when I'd be able to talk about the tree, and somehow, we got to today. I must have agreed to the time. Or I did something, or I didn't do something to stop it. Eventually, he and Adam left, and my fingers are still a little twitchy.

The shaky energy's in large part guilt, of course, but there's something excited about it, too. I tell myself I'm ready now, having prepared appropriate responses to tree questions and put a glaze in my hair for extra energy reflection. And when I go downstairs, it's easy to think something's right with the mountain this morning that hasn't been right in a very long time. Everything feels right—weak and a little nauseated, but *right*—with the exception of the knocking on my downstairs window.

Beatrice is standing in the sunshine and not looking

sunny at all when I open the door. She bursts inside and immediately collapses onto the sofa, putting her feet up on the coffee table and gesturing widely to the windows.

"You must have felt it," she says.

"I..."

"The disturbance, around six this morning. Surely you felt it. It got me right out of bed."

I resist the urge to point out my great-aunt's always getting out of bed at six in the morning; she has her toast by six-thirty and arrives at the inn for her first cup of tea before it opens at seven. I look outside, but nothing seems out of place. There's a light on in Annie's office, and the general store next door's just opening. A couple cars are chugging quietly around the square.

"I felt...something," I offer, "but..."

"It's going to be awful."

I swallow around a rapidly-forming lump in my throat. Beatrice is almost as old as the mountain itself and has never been wrong.

"I felt it," she says. "Screaming, anger, betrayal, evil, the mountain..."

I search for yesterday's pumpkin muffins as Beatrice stands and shivers. I'm not sure something like betrayal can be cured even by pumpkin muffins, though. And I start to feel a bit of a cloud descend myself as my aunt paces the store. I plug in the tree in my front window, just in case someone drives by who's not convinced the mountain's about to be consumed by doom and gloom.

But when I turn back to ask Beatrice for details about what the screaming sounded like or how the evil looked, she's back on the sofa, and she's shaking. Her eyes are closed, and her head's bowed. She jumps as I approach, then lurches forward.

"He's gone. *Gone!*" She waves her arms as she rises and stomps across the store to retrieve her coat. Then she's out the door and disappearing into the blinding morning sunshine.

I tell myself I'm only imagining the change in energy as I inventory some candles and prepare for an afternoon's worth of cappuccinos. But I'm feeling the anger, too, when Beatrice returns a couple hours later. It seems to be growing out on the street into a great ball of Piney Mountain vengeance.

Beatrice is jabbing her finger at a piece of paper and making small squeaking noises when she bursts through my door again, this time flanked by Jane and Angela.

"He's really gone," she says. She pushes the paper at me. It's a deed for land on the North side of the preserve, undersigned by Heslein, signed by Mayor Gliel.

It takes me a couple times reading through it to understand our mayor's been working for the other side. I stare at the paper for a while longer before joining Beatrice out on the sidewalk.

People are starting to gather around her in the street,

angry energy radiating outwards as storm clouds roll in over the mountain and block out the sun. And all I saw was sun. Not the sun shining on Gliel in Florida, either, where he's evidently fled. My breakfast muffin churns in my stomach, and I lean back against the window and focus on taking slow, deep breaths.

All I saw, all I woke up feeling, was good, cleansing energy washing over the mountain and a bright future for Piney Falls. Now, I see Lisa as she rushes towards the crowd and feel some relief on her behalf, at least that her fight's over. If the land's already in Heslein's name, at least she has some closure. It means we've lost, of course, but it's still closure.

And I guess, whatever my psychic butterflies think, that in a way, it should be closure for me, too. It's coming up on a year since I saw Harker's great boon. I should be feeling some relief now, some sense that I can give up the responsibility that's always nagged at me. This is the biggest confirmation I could have gotten from the universe that my gift's really gone.

It will hit Jeff first. The factory runoff will poison Harker's soil, drop the price of the land down too low for him to sell. I see him on the other side of the crowd and mumble something at Lisa before hurrying back inside.

Cold air blasts my ankles even as they start to thaw under my jeans, and I toss the rest of my morning pumpkin muffin into the trash. This is one of those inciting events, I can tell, one of those days when everything changes. Maybe things will change for me, too. Maybe I'll go someplace where losing my gift won't bring sympathetic stares from everyone I grew up with, where I can start over with something new.

I close my eyes and lean into the heating vent by the oven, but when I picture Piney Falls, I still see sunshine and hear laughter. Someone who's not psychic at all would have a better shot at predicting the future just by looking out my front window.

Eventually, the crowd dissipates as everyone starts to cram into the pub. The wind's picking up, blowing the bows on the lampposts sideways, and it's starting to sleet. So much for sunshine.

I set aside a few extra cappuccino mixes for Adam and work up the courage to call Jeff just before noon. I'm thankful he doesn't answer, and I leave him a quick message apologizing for not being able to meet with him today, after all. With the Heslein business over, I'm sure Lisa will want to put her full energy into the tree anyway, and I can't imagine facing him now.

*   *

I have a serious headache by the time Beatrice comes by later in the afternoon. It's sleeting harder now, and the rest of the town is holed up in the inn as they plot revenge on Gliel who, I suppose by popular vote, is no longer our mayor.

I get a bad feeling as I watch my aunt shuffle into the

back room. Frowning and shuffling, she looks nothing like the Beatrice I know, a glistening, multi-scarved sorceress who wields energy like a Triton. The betrayal of her oldest friend must have hit her like a sucker punch from the universe.

"I saw you here," she tells me, "hiding."

I do everything I can to assure her I'm *not* hiding, but my great-aunt's been able to read me better than a crystal ball since before I was born. And the way she's looking at me now tells me she's not buying it. So eventually, I change tactics and try to explain why I'm going to quit seeing peoples' futures backwards, why I have to quit seeing things at all.

Beatrice is shaking her head. "You know you couldn't have seen this," she says. She was the one feeling Gliel's energy, and she blames herself for not being open to seeing to his betrayal or she would have known before this morning.

I feel tears welling behind my eyes as I break down some boxes. I don't know why it hits me like this now, in the middle of an ice storm; I've known for a while that I wasn't seeing anything right. This guilt's just been getting worse and worse these last months.

"I didn't see the mountain," Beatrice reminds me. "I only saw Gliel." She thinks there's a good reason we don't have the same visions; it would be a waste of energy, she says, going to two receivers at once. And Beatrice is all about efficiency.

I nod and try to focus on the boxes, but my hands are

still tingly, like they're trying to pick up something else I'd probably read wrong.

"If you saw everything being well here, then it's going to be all right," she says. "You know I see you well."

I force a smile. Beatrice saw me with the gift before my mom knew she was pregnant. It nearly caused a spontaneous miscarriage when she announced this at the dinner table a few weeks before my parents got married.

"And I don't see you leaving. I don't see you losing the gift, either," she says. "I see you *happy*."

I try to say the right things about how I'm okay and how this isn't a crisis for me, but I'm feeling sick to my stomach as I watch her leave.

When she's gone, I make myself a soothing chamomile tea and get to work reorganizing some coffee bags for distraction. Even with all the angry energy floating around the mountain, all the vengeful thoughts directed at Gliel, I can't stop thinking about Jeff.

I get lost in the guilt until I hear his voice calling my name. Then I realize he's actually here, in the front of my store, and I dive under a table.

6

Several hours later, I'm in Adam's pub. I guess there's a time limit on how long you can hide from the universe under a table.

Lisa found me about an hour ago and coaxed me to Adam's by playing the potentially-dangerous-to-herself-friend-needing-supervision card. She burst into my shop wielding an iphone flashlight like a samurai sword, nearly attacked Annie, and then spent the rest of our walk to the pub muttering about socks. Maybe she can sense the snowball demon, too, and it got inside her somehow. Maybe I should have tried to make peace with it when I had the chance.

Since Lisa spent some twenty minutes screaming at a lawyer she locked in the inn's meat freezer, she's been safely confined to a room guarded by Adam. So I decided this was the wrong time to say something to her about decorating the tree.

I feel Jeff's energy wafting this way as he approaches with a bowl of chocolate pretzels and sense the undeniable draw of bad roast beef, that whatever-it-is about Jeff that makes me want to throw up and move closer to him at the same time.

Watching him duck to avoid an overhead beam and crunch his legs up under the table, I can almost see what Lisa sees—a Neanderthal—only Jeff's the most stunning Neanderthal I've ever met. There's a kind of raw, unselfconscious energy that clings to him and grounds everything around him.

My butterflies react accordingly, my stomach lining disintegrating by the moment. But this is how it always is, how it always will be. I know we'll miss each other again somehow, that we'll pass through this holiday and go in different directions like we always do, me with ulcers and him unchanged.

"Think she's crazy," Jeff's saying, about Lisa. "Adam doesn't know what to do." He says it like there's something to be done. Not like Lisa just locked a lawyer in a freezer. He glances over at the staircase like he expects her to emerge at any moment and begin random attacks on the remaining inhabitants of the mountain.

"I was wanting to ask her about the decorations," I say. "I wasn't sure if the lawyer's gone, or..."

Jeff's expression tells me I don't want to ask him anything about the lawyer right now.

"I guess we could wait on the ribbons," I say.

"Ribbons?"

"For the tree."

"Okay." His arm jerks out from under the table, and he snatches a handful of chocolate-covered pretzels from the bowl. He shoves them into his mouth and swallows. He's like a giant chocolate-covered pretzel disposer. You'd think this would be less attractive.

"We don't have to use ribbons," I say.

"No. Ribbons are good."

I glance around the inn and wonder if conversation was this hard before I developed the crush. I wrote up a checklist last night of generic tree questions to ask him— things that aren't controversial, that are topical, that have nothing to do with him or me or all the *us* times we've almost had before.

I try the next topic on the list. "Colors," I say. "I was going to ask you about the colors."

"Dark green."

I look down into my mug of eggnog. I've only had about a third of it. "Um...for the ribbons. Or the ornaments? Do you like red and green? Or gold, maybe? Or blue?" Or something with clashing polka dots, I think, so Lisa's sure to intervene fully and quickly. "We should ask Lisa," I remind him. "I think she'll..."

Jeff reminds me Lisa's just locked a lawyer in a meat freezer and is currently in no position to be consulting on festive ribbons. Then he reaches for another handful of chocolate pretzels. He's saying something about cider when I look up from his arm.

I try a pretzel, too, but it doesn't sit well with the eggnog in my stomach. Jeff nudges the bowl towards me when he asks about lights. Eventually, I'm lulled into a kind of trance as we talk more about the ceremony, the likelihood of snow, what kind of snow it will be this year, and the chances we'll be singing "Silent Night" under a tarp in the hail like the great frozen tree lighting of '03.

Somehow, we make it through the bowl of pretzels. Jeff returns from the kitchen again, this time with bad tidings of cinnamon buns—Adam's completely out of dough—but carrying a tray with a giant slice of chocolate cake and a couple coffees.

Conversation's a little easier with the eggnog finished. Jeff tells me about his favorite pizza place in Oregon and offers me the fudgy side of the cake, and I feel warm and a little crush-drunk. Possibly because he doesn't mention my cursed gift or anything about how I ruined his plans to eat all the good pizza on the West Coast when I bankrupted his family business.

Little miracles seem to have affected the rest of the town, too, by around nine. The backup solar generator must radiate some magic of its own, calming the mountain's residents with the help of the hearty eggnog and lawyer-purging festivities. Some kids are leading carols on the piano in the far corner of the restaurant now. The music's softer, and I think it sounds better over here by the kitchens.

"But you saw that, didn't you?" Jeff asks about Oregon, when he's telling me about bamboo composites. He gets so excited when he talks about bamboo composites, and I can't help but feel excited, too, seeing him this way. "You saw I was going there, and you said I was gonna work with plants."

My stomach butterflies return with a vengeance. "I'm sure I meant trees," I say. Specifically the ones at Harker's that were washed out in the flooding.

He shakes his head. "That isn't what you said, though. You were in third grade, and you said I was gonna do...pretty things, you said, with plants. Building things. And that I was going to the beach."

My face flushes in a way that has nothing to do the eggnog. My gift was less than graceful when I was a kid, and never did get eloquent. I probably said that after falling nose-first into a salisbury steak.

"You...I said that to you?"

"Not exactly. You told Lisa. Lisa told me."

"Oh." I try to laugh this off, but Jeff's expression doesn't change.

"So maybe you saw this coming," he says.

"What?"

"Beatrice, us working together on the tree. Adam said

you might have, uh...not planned on doing it. But you must have seen it coming."

I open my mouth, then try to gulp down a little more of the coffee. It tastes bitter.

It comes out in short, incoherent spurts then, my acknowledgment that Jeff's wasn't my only bad prediction, that I've lost my gift altogether. I tell him about seeing the mountain thriving, the community programs, all the great energy. And then about the dog. In the end, I can't believe I tell Jeff about the dog.

He stares at me for a couple seconds after I finish. "You haven't lost it, then," he says.

"What?" I must not have articulated very clearly. I guess I shouldn't be surprised.

"Your gift. You said you lost it."

"Uh huh."

"But you still see things."

"Backwards," I remind him. Jeff, of all people, shouldn't need to be reminded of this.

His eyebrows crinkle together. "I think you're wrong, Faye," he says.

I don't have the intestinal fortitude just now to argue with him. And then he smiles.

"Let me show you something," he says. "When the road's clear."

He shows me his teeth, and I know this isn't really a choice for me to make. Maybe it's whatever's happened between us before, or Beatrice's fate, or some critical bacterial imbalance deep in my colon Lauren keeps emailing me about, or something even worse. But whatever it is, I know I'd go anywhere with this man.

7

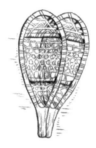

A little over twenty-four hours after waking up in a booth in Adam's pub with Jeff lying sprawled across the floor below me like a beautiful downed tree, I'm trying to cram my feet into snow shoes. The universe is funny like that.

I lace the boots snugly around my ankles and watch Jeff walking ahead of me. Jeff walks about the same in snow shoes as he does in boots, and I see Lisa's verb at work—Jeff *lumbers*—but in a graceful way. Not like a zombie, like Lisa seems to see him.

I stand and wobble in my own snow shoes. The tree farm's blinding in the early morning light. Away from all the exhaust, this part of the mountain always stays a brilliant, shimmering expanse of white until it thaws into April mud. So, when I saw sunshine washing over the mountain, maybe I wasn't as far off as I thought; the sun was just a weather forecast and a couple days early. Unfortunately, timing's everything with psychic predictions.

And now I've gotten so backwards, my energetic compass has hit so much interference, that I think I'm seeing the past instead of the future. It feels like these trees in the new field are the same ones I zipped past on my sled after each tree lighting as a kid, my belly full of Bakeoff cookies and Jeff's dad's special virgin cider. This is the downfall of reading energy without knowing its time, with seeing things in both directions; seeing back, I'm can't imagine leaving the mountain, and seeing forward— or not seeing forward, or whatever it is that's the problem with what I see—I can't imagine how I could stay here.

Jeff's voice brings me back to the present, and I look away from the old sledding routes on the South side of the hill to where he's pointing ahead. Ahead, unfortunately, is straight up a cliff.

I start to smooth my nonexistent skirt, running my hands over the layers of down covering my hips, all this padding that's still not enough insulation between me and Jeff's world. Whatever he wants to show me must be really special since you can only reach it reasonably by parachuting from a helicopter. If Jeff weren't Jeff, I'd suspect he were planning on killing me and burying my body where no one would find it.

He quickly makes his way up the cliff face, which he

describes in his own, significantly more sparse language as a hill. An *icy* cliff face.

As I try to navigate around a tree branch, my snow shoes get off course, and I fall backwards. My butt, the most recent target of the morning snowball demon, hits a sheet of solid ice. And then all I can think, squinting up into the sun, is how I've never heard Jeff laugh like this before.

He reaches out a hand as I push up onto my elbows. Then, when I don't take it right away, he mumbles what he evidently takes to be some kind of an apology, that's really not an apology at all when he's laughing.

I flail around a bit, trying to look as disapproving as an amoebic, blue snow-suited blob can. I finally push up onto my shins. At least all the down filling's worth something in padding.

Once he has his face under control—almost—Jeff reaches for my elbow and hauls me back up with a single pull. My face heats, and I wonder if it will always be like this with him. There's something magnetic about the few feet around him even in freezing winter conditions and through layers and layers of down. I busy myself with brushing snow off my butt.

When I'm finished, Jeff proceeds to haul me up the cliff face before I can get good foot holds on the ice, and I swear he smells like great, sappy tree, all Christmassy and wonderful. Which is probably something even more wrong with me than the dog vision.

I stumble forward when he stops, and it takes me a second to get my bearings. From the top of the embankment, I can see new growth in the expanse of snowy blanket ahead, and I'm surprised by the height of the trees there. Jeff points to the one closest to us.

"A Frasier fir," he says.

I reach out to touch it. Its branches stand out even with the ice weighing them down, and thick, full needles glisten in the sunlight. It looks like it's going to grow up to be the magnificent giant in my favorite children's book, wide and towering and full of singing birds hanging biodegradable garland.

"It's beautiful," I say, in probably the same voice I used on my first visit here as a little girl, the same awe and wonder for that first glorious Frasier fir that graced our living room.

"We got in a crop last year, when we got this field," Jeff says, pointing out that these trees are the same age as the row of spruces on the other side of the hill. "It's the soil here. And the runoff. It washes away the pine needles to keep the acidity down. You told us to get this land."

I shake my head. Not *this* land specifically; I only said Harker's should invest in *more* land, because I saw them falling on some random blast of good fortune that would carry them for several more generations of tree growing. Then they invested in this particular land, and their business went under when the floods came to take out years of trees, new Frasier firs or not. I try to offer Jeff a recap of this in more gentle terms, like maybe he doesn't know it already, but he's shaking his head.

"I'm showing you," he says. "You were right. This plot's perfect for the firs."

I stare into the branches, unsure how to respond. Maybe Jeff's lost it, too. Maybe it's something about the air here. We don't get much oxygen up on the mountain as it is; I imagine a little slip-up in some other chemical could put us into a full-blown fairy gas situation.

I squint into the sun as I scan the trees ahead. They seem to extend forever, little rows of green specs that disappear into the far side of the preserve. The scene looks like a Christmas card. It's just the kind of place built for childhood memories, I think, the kind of place for romantic sleigh rides and hot cider, the kind of place you might expect to tell your grandkids that you fell in love.

I stand there quietly for a while before turning back to look at the old part of the farm. I can feel Jeff's presence next to mine still, this energy I've always been so aware of that in another lifetime could have been a partner, a best friend, someone I might sit on the porch next to and watch generations of trees pushing up through the mud with each spring. I've never been into past life regressions but can't help but feel sometimes like we've already been here and that we've just managed to miss each other this go around.

"I'm working on something," he says. "I'm working on something, and...I think maybe it's okay."

It could just be blood reaching my shins again, but a sudden burst of joy hits me as we stand there afterwards in the quiet. It feels like it's coming straight up from the mountain through the soles of my boots, like the very earth here is happy and hopeful.

We stay there for a while, and whatever it is about the mountain air that's a little hallucinogenic, or maybe just basic oxygen deprivation and being this close to Jeff, makes everything a little brighter. In this moment, leaving Piney Mountain feels impossible.

8

The ride back to Jeff's place is quiet except for the heat hissing out of the air vents. He's been staying in his grandparents' old cottage on the far side of the farm, and we follow his tire tracks in the snow back down the driveway.

I step down from Jeff's truck and am a few feet from my car, ready to drive away, when I hear his voice behind me.

"Come have some cider," he says.

I stop. And I know I should tell him I have get back, should make up some reason I need to return to the relative normalcy of my loft, to get as far away as I can from him and from everything I see here at Harker's.

But I don't say this, don't open my car door. Instead, I

follow him along the little stone path to the cottage. As soon as I step inside, the smell of everything distinctly Jeff washes over me.

He walks ahead of me to the kitchen and gestures for me to take a seat on a wooden barstool as he gets started heating some cider on the stove. It's the first time I've actually been in this cottage, but of course I know it right away—in every vision I've had of him recently, I've seen Jeff here, nestled in this little thicket of trees down the hill from the red storage barn. So this fireplace feels familiar already, and the old wood floors and the cherry cabinets in the kitchen. I get distracted looking around at all these things I've only seen behind my eyelids until now.

"I was thinking we could have it here again," he's saying when I tune back in.

I look up from the orange coils of the stove.

"The sledding," he prompts. "After the lighting."

"Oh," I say.

"I drove around yesterday, and I think the trails are okay."

"It's perfect." I try to say this casually, but I know I'm grinning, and then I feel the joy again, this time wrapping itself around my midsection like an invisible heated blanket.

With everything I love about the mountain and my happy childhood here, none of my other memories can hold a candle to sledding nights at Harker's after the tree lighting. A couple years ago, Jeff's father broke his hip and was taken to a rehabilitative center near family in Raleigh, so Beatrice started doing some kind of snowy treasure hunt around the square for the kids, instead. It was nice, but it wasn't the same.

I try not to think about how this will be the last sledding I'll see before the farm will be sold, probably to Heslein. This is probably the last time the lighting will feature one of its trees, too. I look back at the stove, where the cider's starting to steam.

"I don't know yet about the new sledding paths," Jeff warns me.

I reassure him the old ones are perfect. His sleeve brushes mine as he reaches for the cider mugs, and heat prickles up my arm. It's his energy, an elevated awareness I've always had of it that works like an "off" switch for all the other parts of my brain.

So as the cider starts to bubble, I ask what are probably all the wrong questions about his move from Oregon, about connecting flights and layovers and airport restaurants. By the time he's taking up our drinks, I have a complete logistical understanding of how Jeff, his luggage, and his mail—specifically his mortgage, his utility bills, and at least one sustainable design magazine—get to Piney Mountain.

He hands me a warm blue mug that looks like one of the ones his grandmother made. The cider's hot and tangy on the tip of my tongue, the perfect blend of spice and sweetness that was perfected ages ago, too many generations back to count.

I focus on the little swirls in the liquid when Jeff takes a seat on the barstool across from mine.

"You're being a good sport about this," he says.

"Hmm?"

"I heard..." He pauses, and some cider hisses on the coils of the stove. "I mean because you didn't want to do the tree."

"I..." *was attempting some effort at self-preservation*, my front brain reminds me. Jeff waits, but I don't know how to finish this.

"I'm glad you did it, was what I meant."

I take a bigger gulp of the cider, burning the back of my throat, and feel my skin flush under the wool of my sweater. "Uh huh," I say, then, "Why didn't I want to?"

"It's just, you know, Adam said...working with me..." his voice trails off.

"Adam," I echo, blowing a shaky breath into my mug as I feel Jeff watching me from across the counter. When I meet his eyes again, my head radiates with so much hot energy that I think it might start oozing out my ears.

Then he stands, his palms resting on the counter. "Look," he says. "I'm sorry if I fucked up."

That's when the cider backs up into my nose.

"With you," he clarifies.

I snort some of the hot liquid out a nostril and cover

my face with my hand.

"If I did something to piss you off," he says. "I mean, if I wasn't nice to you or something."

I pull my hand away my face, but no words come out. Probably they'd be laced with flying cider, anyway. If he wasn't *nice* to me? But he looks serious.

I take a deep breath and a deeper sniff. "I don't know what you mean," I finally manage, but in a voice that doesn't sound anything like mine. I take another quick sip of cider to stall the stomach acid ready to erupt into my esophagus. Which now would probably also come out my nose.

Jeff doesn't move. "You do," he says.

Before I can think of a way to deny this, he leans closer on the counter.

"You, you know, don't like being around me. You don't *like* me."

I make some noise of protest, but it doesn't come out with any words that might help me here, whatever those might be.

Jeff looks back to the stove, where some cider's hissing on the coils, then at me again. I look down into my mug, because that feels safest.

"Faye," he says. And I don't know why his using my name always turns my midsection into an active volcano. "You, uh...you ran away from me."

"What? When?" *Which time*, of course, is what I mean, since about the third grade, when I first started running away from him. I never knew he noticed, though. I try not to let my voice indicate just how strong of an urge I have to run away from him now.

"The other day," he says, "on the street."

I continue looking into my cider, thinking maybe I can read the swirls like tea leaves, if I knew how to do that sort of thing. But of course I'm the wrong kind of witch for any of this.

"And, uh, generally, you don't...you've kind of kept away since I came back," Jeff says. "If I did something to upset you, I..."

"I liked you." It's out before I can stop it. "I mean, I had a crush on you when we were younger," I explain, and feel my whole body flush when I look at him again. I guess this is what Beatrice says about the truth not being able to be held inside of us for too long. I didn't think this was how it was going to come out, though, with cider still burning my nasal passages.

Now Jeff has that zombie look he gets sometimes Lisa references, eyes white and kind of bugged.

"You..."

"Had a crush," I repeat, trying to wave my hand dismissively and tapping myself on the nose in the process. And maybe, I tell myself, he'll take this in the past tense like I said it. Maybe he's forgotten about my running away from him as recently as a few days ago. "It was nothing," I say.

He's quiet for a minute, but he looks...amused, and I

think I liked him better when he looked like a zombie.

He sets down his mug. "Are you sure?" he asks after a second.

When I meet his eyes this time, I know I can't make up anything to suggest this was just a mistaken use of the word 'crush.'

"Mmm," I say, focusing on the cider again. If only I could be dangerously attracted to trees or cider or anything, really, other than Jeff. I push my barstool back and pick up my mug, but he doesn't move. Then he smiles, and I decide I definitely like him better in zombie mode.

9

I wake up the next morning from another dog dream with the snowball demon on my butt. Through my window, I can see several tree limbs are down, encased in a layer of ice, and it looks all kinds of freezing outside, the sky gray and cloudy.

And all I feel is sun. But maybe it's a good thing I'm so backwards today; I keep having flashes of Lisa being devoured by a bear.

When I check my phone, it's only seven, two hours before I'm supposed to meet Jeff at her place. He called last night to ask me to come see whatever it is he thinks could save Harker's.

I remind myself to ask Lisa if she's seen any bears lurking around her yard, but my body doesn't seem very concerned about bears, or even about the movement of the snowball demon each morning, which is probably destined to freeze my coronary artery soon.

My mind's still on Jeff, and the snowball demon's nowhere to be found when I squeeze an extra dollop of bubbles into my bath and settle into the tub. These bubbles are a special kind Lauren sent, and I'm counting on their detoxifying powers this morning.

I reach out to make sure my phone still has the alarm symbol on before leaning back against my bath pillow and imagining the water drawing out all my stagnant energy.

But just as I'm thinking about how good the bubbles feel on my toes, light flashes behind my eyelids, and my knees fall to one side of the tub, knocking a bottle into the water.

I try to breathe the vision away, to duck down into the water to heat the vision away, even to shake the vision away, but it washes over me with more strength than anything I've had for several months. I see from the eyes of Lisa's bear just before some kind of sparkly explosion that leaves heat behind. My vision goes black for a moment, when a kind of warm, tingly feeling rushes through all my limbs, and then I see Jeff's cabin, only it's in brilliant color, wavy lines with a splash red in the background.

The feeling lingers well after the vision fades, and I open my eyes to find my bathwater cool and my alarm on its second snooze cycle. I'm shaky as I lift myself out of the tub, and I have to sit down on a stool to dry off.

My legs are still pretty wobbly several minutes later, when I'm dressed and searching for my notebook. I thought I wasn't going to use it again, that it would only be encouraging visions, but this one felt too important not to write down. I raise my pen to a lined sheet of paper after the most recent "dog" page and try to find words for what I felt, what exactly it was that I saw after "bear eats Lisa."

Cider. It felt like cider.

I toss the notebook into my underwear drawer and hope Lisa's bear is at least easier to face than Jeff.

*   *

I get to Lisa's place ten minutes early to find a gray SUV in her driveway and a brand new living room. Lisa does this every once in a while, just sort of disappearing and then, when you least expect it, emerging with a freshly redone room and a happy new perspective like a paint-splattered butterfly emerging from her cocoon.

"You redecorated," I say as I close the door behind me. It looks like this meltdown was a serious one—walls, trim, and furniture in one fell swoop. Lisa's ponytail's half out and pulled to the side of her head, but the bags from under her eyes have cleared, and she's all kind of glowy. And smiling.

"Oh," she says, looking a little dazed, "yeah." Maybe it's one of those urges that just sort of takes over for her and she doesn't know it's happening until she wakes up covered in paint one day. Sometimes, I think of Lisa like a serial killer with dissociative identity disorder who wakes up covered in blood, except with a paintbrush.

I compliment her new fainting couch, and my stomach settles among all the soothing creams and grays. It feels like a totally different place than the cozy, red-walled haven she created in time for the wooly bear festival last year. The tree lights in the corner window reflect brightly off the walls, and whole the room's bathed in a creamy, warm light.

And then Jeff comes in, and all that light suddenly feels too warm. I watch as he crosses the kitchen and lays a plank of wood down on the floor by the fainting couch. He's grinning.

When I look back at Lisa, her hand is over her mouth. Maybe Jeff affects her upper GI, too.

"Woven strand board," Jeff's saying, on his knees now as he lines up another plank with the first.

Lisa pulls her feet up onto the couch and frowns at her floor. She starts to say something about needing another rug but stops short when Jeff lifts the leg of her coffee table and scratches it noisily against one of the boards.

"It's bamboo," he explains. "It's a composite, bound with..." And then there's no stopping him.

I tune out content in favor of just watching, mesmerized, as the mountain's resident of the fewest words tells us about woven strand board and fibers and growing bamboo and making it into whatever it is that looks like wood but that can't be demolished by the legs of the coffee table.

I always knew Jeff was good at working with his hands, at creating things, but this is something new, an eco-friendly material he studied in college and worked on in Oregon. He looks at home holding the boards, and Lisa and I watch silently as he aligns the pieces and links them together, talking about the thickness of the grooves and how much they can bend without breaking and all kinds of numbers that could only mean something to him.

Once a full row's together, he sits back and looks up at us. Lisa studies her newly-assembled floor as I try to focus on it, too, and away from Jeff. Energy radiates out from him, strong and steady like always. He's in his element, you can tell, and I know now *this* is where he belongs, with these boards, whatever I saw or failed to see of him and the tree farm.

And then, as Lisa's running a tentative toe along the edge of her new floor, Jeff's energy shifts. I follow his gaze to the hallway, where a man I don't recognize has just come out of the bathroom. Unidentified males are even more rare than bears on Piney Mountain, and I get a strong feeling about this one that I can't place.

Suddenly, Lisa's off the couch and fiddling with her sweater, and Jeff's facing the intruder and has stepped in front of me. There's a second when they're all three still. There's something, I guess, about Jeff being able to work so well with his hands, in case you ever find yourself facing a strange man lurking in your hallway.

Lisa turns to me, a blush creeping up over her cheeks. "I, uh. You haven't met Kurt Boxler. I don't think."

I stand and feel like my lips are stuck together as I study the man who, of course, I know only by reputation. Jeff hasn't moved, and I wonder how long the lawyer might have stayed locked in Lisa's bathroom to avoid facing him. I think maybe I could have held out for at least a few days.

Kurt glances at Jeff, then extends his hand to me and offers a quick smile. We both mutter something reasonably friendly, considering the situation, but when I take his hand, I have a flash of the light fur from my vision.

"I have some...good news Kurt just brought. Us, actually," Lisa stammers. "Heslein's...Heslein's giving up."

When none of us move, Kurt hurries to the kitchen and returns with some papers. He hands them to me, and Jeff leans closer to look over my shoulder as the lawyer retreats a safe distance to the entryway. With Jeff at my side, I feel like I'm standing in a convection oven.

"So we're not going to have the factory," Lisa tells her

new floor boards, "or the lawsuit, and uh, we have Gliel's cabins...and about seven million dollars."

10

Good news travels fast on Piney Mountain, and Beatrice declared a town holiday within five minutes of the settlement draft making its way downtown. We broke out the pumpkin muffins soon afterwards. This is a symbolic cleansing act, a ritual to purge our minds of our former mayor as we cleanse our colons with pumpkin fiber.

For all the chaos of the last months and the anger that's been swirling around Piney Falls through the week, suddenly, I sense closure. And closure feels good. It's also possible having at least one vision that was accurate feels good. So I'm one for two...or around forty, if you count all the dog dreams. And completely ignore the bear vision and the demonic presence in my living space.

I watch Lisa duck under my Noble Roman's lamp, and she doesn't even pause to glare at it this time as she makes her way to a group of people gathering around her lawyer. She looks euphoric, radiating a bright, happy energy you could almost think was sane, if she weren't oogling a lawyer.

That bright energy seems to be spreading through the rest of the town, too, and it's finally starting to feel like Christmas on Main Street. Someone's plugged in the twinkle lights on my staircase, and Adam's brought over a CD player with holiday music. It looks so much like the Decembers I remember as a kid that you wouldn't even know there's a snowball demon lurking nearby.

Jeff's arm brushes against my side as he opens the oven to check on the next batch of pumpkin muffins.

"This must feel good," he says.

I agree. He means my predictions about the factory, I know, but it's everything else that feels right today.

"I brought you some papers," he tells me then, bending to get a manila folder from a shelf under the cash register. "I wasn't sure you'd understand from just the boards."

When my fingers touch the folder, I get a flash of something that runs like lightening up my arm and through my body, the same feeling of good fortune and prosperity I felt when I first saw Harker's expanding last

February, just before everything went wrong.

I stare down at the envelope for a second before pulling out a sheet of paper that shows the composition of the boards Jeff started installing at Lisa's place this morning.

"And you already saw the trees in the new field," he adds.

I look up from the paper. "You can...recycle? The others?" It's hard to imagine the company surviving several years of trees being lost in the flood, even with the new fields growing so well.

He nods, running his finger down the paper to a diagram. "The sap works with the binding agent, and the needles can be pulverized to stop the mulch from getting too acidic."

I can feel Jeff's eyes on me, that same intensity in the way he looks at everything but that seems to turn me in particular into a kind of energetic supernova. I try to focus on the papers as he explains how he'll convert the unused, flooded portion of the Christmas tree farm to grow bamboo that can be used in flooring and siding and trussing and just about everything else. This way, he tells me, Harker's will have double insurance against failing again.

"So I think we should celebrate," he says at the end.

Before I can agree, Beatrice has swooped in

demanding more muffins.

"I'll be right back," Jeff says, grabbing a platter from the counter to deliver to the hungry townsfolk taking over my store.

I nod, smiling, and try to focus on getting together more drinks. I add enough mix into the machine to make several hot chocolates for the kids, who will be getting out of school on a half day any minute. But my stomach twinges, a stray butterfly flapping around. There's something about the news that's not sitting right in my giddy, energy-overwhelmed brain.

I flip through a couple more pages in the folder, past the woven strand board composition charts and tensile tests to a deed for a plot of land I don't recognize. It's to the bamboo farm in Oregon.

Then my stomach butterfly bursts into a million fanged larvae. Because of course Jeff still has land there, a life there. Piney Falls isn't his home anymore. He'll be back and forth some to manage Harker's, I'm sure, so his parents will have more time to enjoy their retirement, but his life's in Oregon.

When he returns with the empty muffin tray, I tell myself this is how it's supposed to be, that just as I'm starting to feel like I can stay here on the mountain with my gift, Jeff should be where *he* belongs, too, in the heart of sustainable construction country, a kind of bamboo cowboy with a startup to expand and a brilliant life ahead of him. A life he deserves. This is how the universe has always had it; we were never meant to be in the same place for very long.

I remind myself I'm happy for him, and for Harker's, until something cold at my ankles freezes my left foot in midair and I trip into him.

My hand collides with Jeff's chest, and what I see in that moment convinces me I can't do this.

11

There's red paint under my fingernails when I take a step back to study my canvas. I've been wrist-deep in oil paint for the last forty-five minutes, but there doesn't seem to be much color that's actually made it onto the fabric.

When I got an email from an old professor about an art therapy retreat in Roanoke, I didn't think it would involve so much...art. This was supposed to be an escape, a way to lose myself away from the mountain, but now I'm limited to losing myself in paint to avoid a repeat of the spinning wheel incident from yesterday. I guess I'm not very centered this weekend.

"I like your lily," the sculpture artist next to me says. "I don't know how to get that to blend, though," she warns, gesturing to the edges of my canvas. "It's not my medium."

I mumble some kind of thanks, because Kathy doesn't know what *my* medium is, and we talk for a little while about growing flowers at high altitudes. We were instructed to paint a house, a tree, and a person, and that lily Kathy sees on my canvas is supposed to be my person. At least it's a good lily.

I used red for the person because it seems so cheerful, and nude felt inappropriate—risqué, even, in a way I know the woman running this seminar, Joyce, wouldn't have interpreted favorably. Ideally, I need some sort of paint-by-number setup for art therapy projects. I guess my clinical psych degree made me more inclined towards inkblots. Even my clay sculpture was unidentifiable, an abstract spiny thing that merited a much more daunting evaluation than I'd imagined possible. Joyce surmised I was angry and violent, but I'd been thinking of a sunset.

The watercolor artist to my left joins in our gardening conversation with a story about his petunias and a very determined raccoon, and I smile along as I make some more swipes at the canvas.

I thought this would help clear my head, getting away from the mountain for a few nights before the tree lighting, but energy seems to be buzzing around my fingers, and the dog vision's only been getting more clear each night.

We continue talking about petunias and the early frost this year as I try to cover my lily-person with the base of the house itself, eventually painting over the whole side of the canvas with a tree, or at least some slashes of green and brown. Then, when the others turn back to their work, my painting grows. It starts with little dashes of color here and there and slowly melds into something else altogether as I lose myself in my thoughts.

I'd hoped that if I took a break from physically seeing Jeff in the days leading up to the tree lighting, my mind would get some distance, too, and I'd have a better chance of not seeing him in my head anymore after he's gone back to Oregon.

This is the problem with being able to see something in the future that you know can't be. Until this weekend, I thought being wrong was the worst thing that could come from my gift, but when my palm collided with Jeff's chest, he was *all* I could see, and I just keep seeing him, no matter how hard I try not to. He'll be gone soon, back to Oregon and bamboo, and I know I'll still see him even with all this space between us. Sometime in the future, the universe will push us together and then separate us again, over and over, like moons on different orbits.

When I step back from my canvas, a house has taken shape in a small clearing—a cabin in wavy lines with a big evergreen out front that's totally engulfed my lily-person.

There's a splash of red in the far corner, the storage barn. It's Jeff's place, of course, and probably only could be.

When we all set our pictures up on the easels in the front of the room, my eyes keep being drawn back to the cabin.

Joyce starts to explain how she interprets them. "This is all," she says for at least the fifth time today, flipping her afghan for dramatic emphasis, "a projection of your mind."

I glance around at the other attendees, who are practically on the edges of their stools in anticipation. I think art's an important creative outlet and therapeutic in its own right, but this has all seemed a little woo woo to me. Not that I'm in a particular position to be calling anything anyone else does woo woo. Maybe I'm just resentful that it doesn't seem to have helped me; it's supposed to be so therapeutic.

"And the roof," Joyce is saying now, brushing her fingers across the side of an easel, "is your fantasy life." As she proceeds to explain the implications of more and less detailed roofs for our hopes and dreams, I study my own snow-covered roof.

"Is this missing a roof?" she asks, turning to me instinctively as she passes my cabin.

"It's snow," I tell her.

"Oh." She moves on, evidently not ready to tackle

whatever snow on a rooftop means about my psyche.

"This person is very open," she says, pointing out the excess of windows on a recent art grad's whimsical painting of a castle. "And this person has a fragile ego." She stops at the petunia grower's portrait. "The house has thin lines. And you care for family life," she says, pointing out the small size of the house.

He frowns, which is all the encouragement she needs.

"We often see bars on windo. s like this from children who are institutionalized," she tells us. "Because they feel trapped."

"But those are muntins," the petunia grower says.

Joyce nods. "Of course."

He turns to me. "Really, they are," he says. "My parents built that house."

I nod sympathetically and listen as Joyce manages to read childhood insecurity into a Victorian and a split personality into a willow tree. *A willow tree.* I must have missed a lot since graduation. I should have brought Lisa along for moral support, but I sent her an email, instead, and left her to the tree decorating.

"And...what happened to your person?" Joyce asks, turning back to me.

"He's inside the house."

"He?"

"Generic," I say. Because, you know, my neighbors thought he was a flower.

"Oh." Joyce eyes my tree for a second before returning to my painting's missing person. "Can you tell me a little bit about him?"

"He's a dog."

She opens her mouth, and the watercolor artist makes a kind of hiccup beside me.

"He's been on my mind a lot recently," I admit.

12

I'd planned an extra day of post-conference soul-searching and inner energy-calming in Roanoke, but the dog vision hit me again in the middle of the last session. So I stopped at every coffee place between Roanoke and Radford and let the stupid dog drive me back up the mountain.

I pass the turnoff to the square and pull into my driveway, trying to keep the giant Christmas tree down the road out of my mind at least until tomorrow afternoon.

It's almost six when I climb the stairs to my loft. I sit for a while just staring out the window then, mentally preparing for the next day and a half of sound checking and tree lighting and sledding and whatever comes after that. Jeff will stay in town through the holiday, I'm sure, through the Bakeoff and the Pageant, and probably through Adam's new year's luau. We're bound to pass each other a few more times after tomorrow.

I focus on pushing Oregon and bamboo farms and *him* from my head, on getting back to isolating the dog in my subconscious and squeezing it out through my ears like a giant, slobbery psychic parasite. I even lie down and close my eyes for a few minutes, but I can't seem to meditate or sleep, and all I can see behind my eyelids is the stupid dog. And then the snowball demon settles on my stomach. Steven will probably be wanting me to swallow some serious pills soon.

After a few minutes of failed meditation, when I'm finally giving into the madness and focusing on making peace with both the dog and my loft's resident snowball demon, I decide to try to walk the vision out, ignoring the blinking red light on my answering machine as I shove on my snow boots and parka. There's something about cold mountain air and the quiet of nighttime that should be cleansing. And, if it's possible to *freeze* out a vision, Piney Mountain in December should be the place to do it.

Main Street's still lit up, though it's quiet when I close the front door of my shop and step out from under the awning. The heavens are clear tonight, and I know I could see a million stars if I were just a little farther away from the square. I think of Jeff, who should be able to see every star in the sky from his cabin tonight. I consider driving there and apologizing for leaving without letting him know, or saying something else. But there's not a point, really, nothing in the future that this would change. And he's not expecting me until tomorrow.

I walk past the vet's place, her front window now sporting a wooden dog wearing a Santa hat, and the post office. When I step down from the sidewalk and onto the big lawn, I see the tree right away. It's giant this year, bigger than any other I remember, and I can tell even from all this distance away that Lisa's had no hand in decorating it.

Cold air stings my eyes as I will my feet forward. Ribbons of all colors are hanging from the lower branches in little bows and mismatched chains. The tree's dark, but when I get close, I can make out the text on a hood of glass tied to a sturdy branch. It's a Noble Roman's lamp. I reach out to touch it. There are more of them winding up to the top in a kind of spiral up to the snowy heavens.

"Do you like them?"

The lamp sways, and a branch snags the elbow of my parka as I spin around.

Jeff steps down off a ladder leading to the platform for the musicians.

"Lisa was..." I start, but he's shaking his head.

"I thought she was gonna have a fit. Beatrice stopped by this morning and said I should go ahead with our plans, and I remembered we hadn't really..." He looks at the ground, then back at me. I can't make out his face. The street lights are too far away, and the moon isn't high enough yet. But the snow seems to glow under us, shooting energy up through my boots that I think could send me straight up into the night sky like a rocket.

My eyes settle on the lamp as my heart pounds a steady beat in my ears. This tree feels more magical even than all the ones when I was a little girl, when I still believed that the universe's plans were good. And the lights aren't even on yet.

"I got the lamps early," Jeff says after a second. "When Lisa said you were gonna replace yours, I thought she meant you needed a new one. So I called a contractor friend of mine who just redid one of those places in Indiana, and he had these. Lisa wasn't too happy about it."

"They're perfect," I tell him when I have control over my voice. It's *all* perfect, and I decide right now that this his exactly how I'll remember this moment when I come back here in my memory, isolated from whatever comes next and like there never was anything that came before it.

"Beatrice said…"

"Beatrice," I interrupt. "She was supposed to be out of town."

Jeff takes a step closer. "Must've been a mistake. She said you were going somewhere, too, that she saw you leaving."

I try to swallow. My mouth's gone dry.

"She said you were running away."

In my peripheral vision, he takes a couple more steps, and my stomach reacts accordingly. I swear I can smell him even out here with the breeze and the tree and everything else. He doesn't say anything for a while as I run a branch between my fingers.

"You saw the roots?" he asks then. "Adam helped me dig it up Saturday. So we can replant it where Heslein's already taken down some trees at the site."

I nod, and tears sting my eyes, freezing there in the wind. "I think Lisa would like that," I say, trying to smile.

"The sledding paths are all ready, too." He gestures back to Harker's land, then drops his hands. "Faye, are you running away?"

It's my name that does me in. My stomach lurches, and I want to say that it must have been a mistake, that for the first time, Beatrice may have been wrong. I open my mouth, but nothing comes out but a breath of steam.

When I finally do find some words, they sound weak, wrong. Because Jeff doesn't know how much I've thought about all the places I might go after the holidays, about all the ways I might try to shake myself free of visions of everything I've seen wrong, but mostly of him.

He's quiet as I stare into the branches, tears building behind my eyes, but I can still feel him here beside me, hot cider and so much more.

He steps around to my side, and my hands go instinctively to smooth the skirt that isn't there anymore. It feels like the rest of an old skin has come off of me, too.

"I don't want to run away," I say before I know I'm going to say anything at all.

I think I knew it before I went to the retreat. I was trying to cope with the idea that I belonged here, for the first time it was something I'd had to cope with. Because when my hand collided with Jeff's chest, I felt his arms around me, hot apple cider on snowy Christmas nights in his cabin and everything else that can't happen in this world. I lose myself in this vision that feels almost like a memory, and I'm floating somewhere overhead when he touches my shoulder.

"I was hoping you'd stay," he says.

His voice is soft, but I hear it like it's coming through the trees, from all around us. I stay for a short eternity in this moment, feeling it wash over me and rain down into the soil to become part of the mountain itself, of our shared history here.

A car driving around the square brings me back to now, a little rumble in the distance.

"When are you going back to Oregon?" It's out of my mouth before I can stop it, and I wish I could postpone asking this question through Christmas and just hold onto this feeling until he's gone.

Jeff drops his hand from my shoulder, and suddenly, I regain feeling in my stomach. What stomach I have left. I turn away. I want to walk straight through the middle of the tree, to be lost in its branches like I was as a little girl under the orchestra stand late at night, listening to the cheers and the boards creaking under the musicians' feet.

"I'll have to go back a couple times a year. But I think most of the work should be done locally. Here." He runs a boot over some red tarp acting as a tree skirt. "It feels like home to me, too, you know."

As my stomach processes this information and my skin starts to buzz with whatever alien energy it's been picking up recently from the great beyond, probably from some cosmic canine realm, Jeff tells me there are some good sledding paths in the new part of the farm, after all, and about adding something of his own to the cider recipe this year, starting a new tradition.

"I was just gonna go start making it," he says, gesturing behind him, where Piney Falls ends and Harker's begins. "I only came by to bring the star."

It takes me a few seconds to convince my legs to move. I'm warm all over, though, as I follow him to the platform, where a lopsided paper mache sphere with a light bulb at its center is sitting in a cardboard box. He holds it out for my inspection, and I run my fingers over the words. It's a draft of Heslein's settlement offer, art therapy at its best.

"We've signed it?" I ask.

"Beatrice had everybody in town put their names on it." He points to an empty spot in the middle. "We left a space for your name here."

I agree it's the perfect star, for the perfect tree, and we stand looking at it for a while before I work up the courage to speak again. "Do you want a hand with the cider?" I ask.

Jeff looks at me with that smile I always see when I close my eyes. "I'd like that," he says.

So we turn back to Main Street, my stomach full of butterflies and the rest of me full of the psychic version of fairy gas. But my stomach, my ankles, and everything else are perfectly warm.

I gesture to where my car's parked in the lot behind my shop.

Jeff shakes his head. "I'll drive you," he says.

I agree, after a second, stomach or no stomach. Probably no stomach, by the end of it. I unwrap my parka as we walk to where he left his truck at the end of the square, and the wind doesn't seem to touch me.

He opens my door before walking back around the hood, and something big and dark licks the left side of my cheek. Its breath is warm and smells like bacon.

Jeff jumps into the truck and spins around to contain the dog in his back seat. "Sorry," he says, "*Down*, Tuffy!"

The charcoal-colored pit bull lunges forward again, going for my neck this time.

"Sorry. I just got him. He doesn't like to be left at home."

I watch, unable to move, as the dog from my visions

licks my hand.

"Sorry," Jeff repeats. "He has a thing about that, too. Toothless, *down*." His hand brushes mine when he tries to haul the animal off me. "Toothless was his old name. It's kind of a long story."

I nod, tears stinging my eyes.

My hand settles on Jeff's when the beast sets his paw on the console between us and we both reach for him. As he tries to block Tuffy/Toothless from jumping forward again, I leave my hand there.

I can see so much more, and everything so clearly this way. When I close my eyes, I hear laughter and see sledding on the new trails. I feel the warmth of the fireplace in his cottage and know this Christmas brought me extra gifts.

Christmas with the Dog

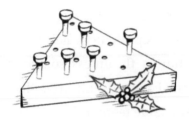

Annie

When I set Cracker Barrel's triangle peg game on the shelf next to my DVM certificate, this odd little space feels more like a home. The peg game has stuck with me through all my dinners at Cracker Barrels on the road with my family as a kid and then later, on my own. I think about all these places I only called home for a little while.

This should have been just another one, another floorplan and grocery store and pizza delivery that are all about the same everywhere, but ascending Piney mountain was like boarding the Neighborhood Trolley and being transported into very cold, very strange Mr. Roger's Neighborhood. Except with more sweets and a lot more snow. And *so* many neighbors.

Fortunately, so far, not one of these neighbors seems

to suspect I'm running from the law. I look at Toothless, his sweet smile oozing drool as he snoozes on the mattress on the floor of my future waiting room.

The paws of my cat clock graze by six-thirty in the morning. This is at least the third six-thirty I've seen this week, in the dark and cold that will stay long into the new year. It's not Toothless and his aggressive cuddling that's messing with my sleep, though; he's the kind of dog you know couldn't hurt a fly unless someone he loved was being threatened. I named him after the misunderstood dragon with retractable teeth in *How to Train Your Dragon*, and I was hoping the judge would see him that way, too.

Unfortunately, there's something about a pit bull bite that's different from a corgi or a chihuahua bite, or even from a horse bite, even though all evidence pointed to the man Toothless bit having been in the process of harming his son. The judge put the son in the protective custody of Child and Family Services, but he still sentenced Toothless to death.

Toothless came to me in a cage wheeled in by an animal control officer, needing stitches from wounds on his back and a few weeks of antibiotic treatment for a collar that had become embedded in the skin of his neck. He'd been chained outside his whole life. The officer informed me his status was pending a legal investigation, and I hoped the dog-fighting bastard would be stabbed to death in jail before it could be completed.

To his credit, Toothless was more forgiving. He laid quietly while we worked on him, tail thumping on the table, and he eventually got free rein of the boarding suite with one of the vet tech's parakeets, Crackers, whom Toothless allowed to ride around on his head. So I want to say I was surprised when the judge ordered him to be euthanized. I testified on his behalf. I petitioned the court. I did everything I could think of to do. But in Brooklyn, a pit bull's a pit bull, and that was that.

When he was scheduled to be put down, the owner of the clinic and all the vet techs were off ·on long Thanksgiving weekends with their families, and I was staying late in the emergency clinic. So I signed the court paper saying I'd euthanized the dog, left my resignation on the front desk, and hid Toothless in my apartment until I could figure out where to go next.

It was probably time to move on, anyway. I'd been in Brooklyn for almost eight months, and I've done this so many times before without the defiance of a court order: I respond to an opening when a vet goes on maternity leave or a clinic needs some extra help. I rent the same kind of pay-by-the-month apartment, treat the same kinds of pets in the same kinds of places. Then I move on to the next one.

It's a lifestyle I've gotten used to. I like the after-hours shifts, the overnights in emergency clinics by myself, the free work for low income owners, the moving on. I find I'm suited to it, that I'm one of those people who can blend in as well in Brooklyn as in Oregon and who you think looks just like five other people you know, with my hamster-colored hair and average build and starkly normal features that don't belie any interesting origins.

My parents, off on their more adventuresome world travels, have been encouraging me to open my own practice for years—to set a stake in the ground, to settle down somewhere, to have a home. Then, with Toothless, I really didn't have much choice, since most apartments don't accept pit bulls.

I spent a week looking for impersonal little town offices to rent before I found this place. And, for the first time in weeks, something went right; Piney Falls is one of the last places on the planet the court might go looking for a fugitive dog. For one thing, I don't think many in law enforcement have what it takes to climb the mountain.

Toothless sits up and drools on my sleeve, and I scratch his ears. This is our fifth morning in the waiting room, and I wish I could let him out into a bigger space to play. He's spent most of the last day or so with his nose pressed against the back window, since I have to hide him from Main Street during the days. Soon, I'll start clearing out the attic to make a little loft for us.

The paws of my wall clock tick past six thirty-five as I put some boxes away. Since no sane person is out yet in the cold, I don't panic when Toothless takes his wet nose to the front window to survey the sleepy town. I tell him this is a good home for us, at least for a little while, as I sit back down on the mattress.

And then a Neanderthal falls through my ceiling.

*   *

After the commotion of taking off his shoes and coat to calm down Toothless, the Neanderthal's holding his boots in one hand and looking at me like *I* just jumped out of the ceiling.

"Gliel said you'd be at the inn," he says.

"I...was going to." My voice reeks of guilt, and then I start babbling about unpacking, about needing to put in some new shelves, about anything but the pit bull currently pushing his nose into the Neanderthal's crotch. And here I am trying to explain myself to someone who jumped out of my ceiling at six thirty-five in the morning.

"The upstairs isn't done," he says. "You can't sleep there yet."

Actually, I can't seem to sleep *anywhere*, but he doesn't need to know that. When I ask who he is, he looks at me like part of being a Piney Falls townsfolk is dropping unexpectedly through ceilings in the wee hours of the morning while I'm trying to redecorate in my onesie. He eyes me warily for a moment—maybe it's the onesie—before gesturing to the ceiling.

"Jeff," he says. "I'm doing the solar panels and getting rid of the duct work."

"Duct work," I echo. When this funny little town's

mayor told me the place needed some work done before I could fully move in upstairs, I thought someone would, you know, *call* first.

"The ducts, they're....what makes it hot or cold," the Neanderthal tells me. "There's a better way to make the ventilation..."

"I know what ducts are."

He shrugs. "Okay."

"Did I, um...hire you?"

He shakes his head and says something about doing work around the square since he's home, something about efficiency, and then about solar panels. I have no idea what 'home' means to him, and I hope he doesn't mean *here*, like I've just inadvertently leased an office and a loft before meeting its resident Neanderthal ghost, who also happens to do duct work.

He looks pointedly at Toothless. "You have a dog."

"Uh huh," I say, automatically, then, "He's not mine."

Toothless whines in ecstasy as Jeff scratches the meaty part of his head.

"Adam didn't say you had a dog."

"He's not mine," I repeat. "He belongs to...to someone else." Like the government.

"Not on the mountain."

I shake my head. I've always been a bad liar. So I take a deep breath and tell myself breaking and entering is worse than pit bull euthanasia falsification. It probably isn't, though, to the court.

"You're sleeping here with the dog," he repeats.

"He's not used to sleeping alone."

Jeff continues rubbing Toothless's head, and Toothless closes his eyes in evident doggy bliss.

"He's afraid of shoes," he says.

"That's right."

"He's a pit bull. Was he a rescue?"

"Uh…huh."

And when the Neanderthal looks up from Toothless's head, I can tell he sees right through me.

2

The next morning, Jeff still has all the grace and charm of a wooly mammoth. Apparently, he also has a key to my office. Not that he needs one, since he can just pop in through the ceiling whenever he likes.

"So you're blackmailing me," I say.

He stands quietly for a moment, which he seems to do a lot, then nods. Earlier, he informed me I had to go to lunch with someone named Beatrice. I told him I already had lunch plans—you know, a perfectly yummy microwavable Amy's veggie lasagna from the little freezer behind the front desk.

Then he asked if anyone else in town had met Toothless yet.

I wanted to call his bluff, but I can't read early

Cromagnon microexpressions well enough to know if he was bluffing.

"Why does she want to have lunch with me?" I ask.

Jeff shrugs. "She just told me to get you." He says it like it's some natural law of the universe that one just does what Beatrice commands, and I wonder what kind of creature could possibly have this power over him. He says her name with the sort of reverence I'd expect him to reserve for saber-toothed tigers.

"How do you know her?" I try.

"Faye's great aunt."

"And Faye's..."

"Faye." He points to my front window like he expects Faye to appear there. Or maybe Faye *is* my front window. Or a lamp post, or some other inanimate object.

"The psychic," he prompts.

"Psychic?"

Jeff's eyes narrow, and I stifle my laugh in case he engages in some sort of ritualized cult veterinarian sacrifice.

"Beatrice is psychic, too," he says.

So it *is* some kind of a witch commanding the Neanderthal. "Oh," I say, because I don't know what else to say. "Okay. But can you tell her I'm busy unpacking?"

Jeff shakes his head, turning to the door as someone else who shouldn't be in my office knocks, then walks in. I thought the "closed" sign would offer adequate protection, but apparently signs and doors don't work on this mountain.

I glance anxiously towards the back room, where I've locked Toothless, and hope the Trans-Siberian Orchestra music blasting on my CD player there masks his noisy tail thumping.

This intruder's carrying a stack of magazines and looks nothing like the Neanderthal. In fact, if I thought it were possible, I'd say he's the first normal person I've seen on this mountain. He's an average height with an unassuming haircut, unstartling clothes, and a warm smile.

Steven, as Jeff introduces him, extends his hand and flashes dimples that make him look much less average up close.

As Steven sets the magazine pile on the counter, there's an ominous *thunk* of something falling off a shelf in the back room. An electric guitar solo masks what I'm sure is Toothless scarfing down the tin of sugar cookies my parents sent up from a bakery in Radford.

Steven frowns. "Are you seeing patients already?" he asks.

"It's bad vents," Jeff tells him. "I'll have it taken care of soon."

Steven nods, and Jeff bids us goodbye as he closes the front door of the my office like a civilized human being who knows how to use doors.

Alone with Steven, I summon my limited conversational skills and take this opportunity to ask him about Beatrice. He explains in a vague but still pretty ominous way that the woman sending messengers to make sure I join her for lunch and am supplied with plenty of magazines for my waiting room is a gifted sort of witch with an equally gifted witch grand-niece. I may have inferred the witch part.

Steven apologizes for the limited magazine selection, all the headlines on heart health and new cholesterol drugs. He identifies himself as a cardiologist and tells me about his upside down tomato plants and the town's Bakeoff in a couple weeks, which Beatrice always wins, just before the Christmas Eve pageant.

It's the way you talk to put someone at ease, when they're not a dog and you can't just ruffle their ears, that special adaptation some people have to show you they're nonthreatening. I note the pauses when he looks at me and hears my questions, this focus he has that probably makes him a great doctor. I get the feeling Steven's the kind of person who sees more than he says.

I realize somewhere in the middle of the conversation, when I'm wondering why anyone would grow tomato plants in December, and upside down, that I'm enjoying talking to him. I want to think it's because he's the only other sane person I've met so far in Piney

Falls and he didn't come through my ceiling. It's not just that, though. It's something in his manner, something easy and kind.

Attraction's science. I know the chemicals and the mating dances and how reproduction and loss and heartbreak work. I've dated at least a little over the years, enough to know this surge of chemicals at the beginning isn't what sustains a relationship.

So I'm surprised when I try to keep this going, asking more about Steven's tomato plants. I watch as he uses a spare *Men's Health* order card to diagram the proper grow light and water reservoir position.

"I'll bring you some when they're ripe," he offers. "They're the kind you'd use for grilled cheese."

"Grilled cheese?"

As Steven fills me in on the town's unique culinary traditions—which consist of the inn's renowned cinnamon sticky buns, fried bologna sandwiches, and grilled cheese with tomato slices, apparently thanks to a past resident—I wonder if I'm starting to feel the effects of the altitude here. Or maybe it's just that the people I'm used to talking with talk mainly about intestinal parasites and laser surgeries.

"Do you have family here?" Steven asks. "Nearby, I mean."

I give him the my-parents-are-overseas story and explain that I don't have siblings, cousins, and so forth in the area.

"So you came here, just…"

"Randomly." I force a *no-your-cat's-delightful* smile. Over the long drive here, I tried to put together some coherent reason why I'd move to Piney Mountain, something other than it being a perfect place to hide a pit bull and avoid being found in contempt of court. But I still haven't come up with anything credible.

When I ask about his roots, Steven tells me that, like Faye, he also has a great-aunt in town who stirs up a lot of trouble, only his is evil.

"You'll be able to see her place from upstairs," he tells me, pointing towards the back of the building. "You know she's baking children up there when there's smoke coming out the chimney."

I laugh, creasing the corner of a *Prevention* magazine. Is that my laugh? It must have been a while since I've laughed. I try to modulate my voice as the discussion turns to Christmas again and Steven brings my attention to my front window. I knew there was going to be something wrong with it when Faye turned out to be a real person.

"We put up trees last Tuesday," he says. "Since you're just settling in, I thought you might want one."

"A tree?"

"It doesn't have to be a Christmas tree." he says. "I mean, if you don't celebrate Christmas, it could be a Hannukah tree, or an Eid tree, or a cat tree, or whatever you want. We usually turn them on at five. And then next week's full indoor lights, and then after the tree lighting, it's outdoor lights, and then ceiling displays three days before Christmas."

I look out the window as I try to process this. I must need more sleep. Not that I was ever great at talking to men about anything other than parasite prevention and species-appropriate nutrition before this.

"I could bring you one if you want," Steven offers. "So you're not left out. I keep just a little twig tree at my office in case of emergencies."

I have no idea what kinds of emergencies in a cardiologist's office might be thwarted by a twig tree, but I stammer through a thank you.

"And don't worry about the ceiling display," he tells me. "Adam always keeps some extra reindeer. I'll let Jeff know he can use one of those when it's time."

I don't know how to thank him for this, so I settle on a nod. Of all the places I've lived, no one's ever offered to bring me a reindeer before.

Steven promises to check in with me later this week so he can set up a time to bring the tree around.

There's a crash in the back room as he's leaving, and he frowns as he turns from the door. "Was that the vents, too?"

"It's nothing," I say. There's some clanking as I imagine Toothless chews up another tin of something. "Jeff's taking care of it."

Steven nods, wishing me happy settling in and telling

me to call him—because apparently everyone knows everyone else's number on this mountain—if I need anything.

He waves through the window as I click the lock behind him, and the pit bull scratching at the door of my back room reminds me I shouldn't be thinking about forming any new relationships here.

3

Without all her scarves, the infamous Beatrice looks like a cross between Mrs. Claus and Betty White. Her white curls spring into place once she's unwrapped her innermost scarf.

She readjusts her spectacles and smiles at me from across the booth. I'm pretty sure it's meant to be a comforting smile, but I can't seem to shake the feeling she's not a harmless kind of witch.

"We're just delighted you're here," she says, pushing a gooey cinnamon bun towards me. "You're going to love living on the mountain."

I try to smile. It's hard to say whether this is a town motto of some kind of a prediction. I can at least agree that it's a nice community—so nice, in fact, that what I gather is the entire town has already been by to visit me, or at least leered into my front window for an uncomfortably long period of time.

"It must be tough living downstairs until your loft's finished," Beatrice continues. "I know Jeff's been there to take care of your ducts. Isn't Jeff wonderful?"

Considering she's talking about the man who blackmailed me into attending this lunch and thinks it's totally acceptable to come through my ceiling in the wee hours of the morning when I'm still in my onesie, 'wonderful' isn't exactly the word that comes to mind. But I decide it's best not to contradict the witch.

"I heard he's doing solar panels, and some...uh, energy things around town," I say.

Beatrice nods, grinning as she tells me about the west coast eco wonderfulness Jeff's bringing to Piney Falls.

"We're going to be entirely on alternative energy within ten years," she says proudly. "And of course you've met Lisa?"

I nod. "She brought me candy bars in a beautiful blown glass bowl yesterday." Lisa, Steven warned me ahead of time, is the town's interior designer. I'm glad he warned me; I've never had anyone sneak-rearrange my furniture before.

"She'll decorate your office when you're ready," Beatrice promises. "She's excellent."

"That's...great."

"And have you met my niece? Faye?"

"I don't think so." Though I did think she might be my front window for a little while.

Beatrice waves a hand, bright jewels flashing on her fingers. "You will soon," she says. "And you've met Steven." This one doesn't sound like a question, and she looks at me for a long moment before taking another bite of her sticky bun.

"Of course," she says, blotting her lip with a napkin. "And did you know we have a lawyer in town now?" Her attention's ostensibly focused on the sticky bun as she cuts it with her fork.

Does she know, I wonder, that I need a lawyer? *Do* I need a lawyer? I haven't heard anything back from Toothless's judge or from Brandon, the owner of my last clinic. I assume they found the paperwork all right and haven't needed Toothless's head to do a rabies test for Mr. Dog Fighting Bastard, but even the gooey wonderfulness of the sticky bun doesn't sit well in my stomach when I think about this. It's like parental paranoia, only for a pit bull without legal rights. So much worse.

"He's very handsome," Beatrice says, about the lawyer.

I open my mouth to say something that indicates I'm not interested in any handsome lawyers—because no one's really interested in lawyers, handsome or otherwise, unless that person happens to be an outlaw, which I am only partially, and I hope only temporarily—but she waves a hand to stop me.

"He's not for you, I mean, but he's a good man."

"Oh. That's...good."

She nods. "Just in case you ever need one. He flew in for the Heslein business. You've probably heard about the factory already?"

I admit I haven't heard of any factory, and she tells me a little about the town's fight against some sort of plastics corporation trying to destroy the wilderness preserve around the mountain.

"You saw the PA?" she asks at the end.

I look at her blankly. I thought I saw some shrubbery in the shape of the state abbreviation for Pennsylvania lit up in the town square when I first got to Piney Falls. But it was late at night and after a long drive, so I attributed it to stress.

Beatrice recounts the intense, three-meeting debate over whether the commissioned shrubbery should honor the town of Piney Falls or the Awe Wilderness Refuge. As she tells me about the town's logo depicting the waterfall, which I initially mistook for a vomiting tree, I look around the inn's dining room and wonder how exactly I got *here* from Brooklyn. There's country Christmas music playing through the speakers and twinkle lights hung around the fireplace and draped over the sides of a baby grand piano in the far corner of the room.

During the briefest time I wasn't concentrating, Beatrice managed to shift our conversation to the town's upcoming holiday pageant.

"You're going to love it," she says.

"It sounds wonderful."

She nods. "It's truly one of a kind. We have menorahs and a song about Eid every year."

I study her face for some sign I'm supposed to laugh, but she looks serious.

"And it's the perfect way for you to meet everyone," she says.

I feel anxiety at the thought there might be more *someones* in this town than I've already met as Beatrice continues to describe the pageant in all its quirky charm. Or at least what she seems to think is its charm.

"He lives closer to Radford," she's saying now. "You'll need to get together to discuss the script, and I'm sure you'll want to see the city while you're there. And he can show you his tomatoes."

"Pardon?"

"Steven," Beatrice says. "He'll be your co-director. He's growing upside-down tomatoes in his office. He has grow lights. LED's."

I try to locate the point when this conversation went wrong. Then, when I can't remember, I run through every excuse I can think of for why I can't be part of a holiday pageant, charmingly multicultural or not.

My reasons are shot down methodically and with alarmingly little effort on the old witch's part—my schedule won't be affected because everyone knows their parts and is flexible, there are only two rehearsals beforehand, and excellent cookies will be provided. Like, some of the best cookies in Virginia, and probably in the world.

"But I...I wouldn't want to take someone's job," I try.

Beatrice beams. "We alternate."

I make a few more comparatively feeble excuses about my lack of experience in theater and how I can't be sure I'll be spending the holidays in Piney Falls. But of course my lack of prior experience will lend the pageant the fresh vision it so desperately needs, Beatrice tells me, and she's already seen that I *will* be in Piney Falls through the holidays. In fact, I'll be here for the psychic-foreseeable future, so I'd best get unpacked.

By the time Beatrice is discussing prop options for this year, which includes a flying Star of David, I've run out of excuses—except, of course, for the one about why I don't make friends when I move. This I learned from years of being a military brat and then moving around after vet school. I've never been anyplace long enough to outstay a gerbil. And if anything goes wrong with Toothless's forged paperwork, I'm gearing up for life as the country's first nomadic veterinarian since caveman days. Though I'm pretty sure cavemen didn't keep pets, even gerbils.

Before I can work up the nerve to do any more

protesting, Adam, the innkeeper, returns to take our orders, and I realize I haven't touched my menu.

"The fried bologna's the best," Adam tells me after Beatrice has ordered some soup and another cinnamon bun. "Or the roast beef. It's an old recipe Lucy's husband left me when he passed away. He built the inn."

"She should try the broccoli casserole," Beatrice says.

Adam shrugs, and I watch inertly as he takes the menu from my hands. He stays to chat for a couple minutes, asking me about Jeff's progress on my duct work and how I'm adjusting to Piney Mountain life. I don't know what to say when he asks what brought me here.

"No family," he says. "Just a lucky accident, then?"

"That's it," I say. *Lucky.*

Beatrice waits until he's out of earshot, then smiles as she turns back to me. "How long have you been a vegetarian?" she asks.

I open my mouth. Nothing comes out.

"And dear," she says, reaching across the table to pat my hand, "no one gets *anywhere* by accident."

4

The next day, I listen to my voicemail one more time as my cell phone beeps to signal it's running low on battery. It started icing around noon, when the mob out in the street finally started to break up, and the power's been out for a few hours now. I'm assuming the zombie apocalypse has just reached Piney Mountain. Or it might have started here.

Annie, it's Brandon. I'm calling about some paperwork an officer came by about today with that pit bull you put down before you left. I'm sure it's no big deal, but he wants to talk to you. They can't find the rabies test.

I fast forward through the hope-you're-settling-in-well-in-your-new-practice pleasantries and then click on Brandon's second message as I try to contain my lunch.

Annie, it's me again. I got a call from the court today, and the prison doctor found the bite wounds were deeper than they thought and needs that rabies test. I don't know if the guy's sick or what. The officer on duty said he didn't have the dates, but they didn't think you had the dog more than two weeks for quarantine. The lab must have mislabeled the test. I know the paperwork's a pain when you're moving, and I hope everything's okay. Call me when you can.

Toothless looks up from where he's lying across my legs like an oversized chihuahua. Of course the rabies test isn't there; his head is still firmly attached to his body. He was only in our office for nine days, but he's not showing any symptoms of rabies or of anything else, and it's well past what would have been his quarantine period now. And why the state of New York would pay for a rabies test for the benefit of someone who fights his dogs and beats his children is beyond me.

Toothless rolls sideways in the blanket I've wrapped around us, leaving a trail of drool over my knee. I don't have a plan. I don't even know what the court's next step is when his head turns up missing. Even in Brooklyn, a pit bull head doesn't just disappear. A veterinary license is another story.

I jump at a loud knock from the back hall. Toothless tenses, and I wrap my hands around his chest. Jeff comes in before I can get to the door.

Jeff already has his shoes in his hands when he reaches the hallway, but he's looking like an overexcited pit bull is the least of his concerns.

"Have you seen Faye?" he asks.

I release Toothless, who jumps up and puts his paws on Jeff's chest. Toothless is a funny kind of guard dog; people who drop from my ceiling are no problem, as long as they remove their shoes, but the existence of what I can only assume is some kind of phantom cat that occasionally wanders by the back window is cause for a full lockdown.

"I haven't," I tell him, and then remember that I've never seen Faye and so have no idea what she looks like. "I don't think so, anyway."

"She's not at Adam's." Jeff pauses, kneeling down to Toothless, who promptly slobbers all over the front of his coat. "Why aren't you over there?" he asks.

"I'm okay. I've been staying pretty warm here."

"Go," he says. "We won't get power back tonight."

I nod, but I'm feeling pretty anti-company at the moment. And I couldn't just leave Toothless alone. Not with an invisible cat on the loose. He'd bark himself hoarse.

"I'll, uh...see how the temperature goes," I say.

Jeff nods, but he's looking at my ceiling. "I'm gonna see if she has candles lit upstairs," he says. Leaving his shoes on the floor for Toothless to gnaw on, he reaches up to remove a tile, then climbs into my ceiling. I wish he'd stop doing that.

When he gets there, he reports that he can't see well enough to get a good look into Faye's windows. Steven mentioned him having a thing for her, and I hope it's not the kind of thing that causes him to try to kill her in her sleep or something. You know, like, with a gun, from my upstairs window.

"Oh," he says, moving something overhead. "I forgot. You need a P.O. Box."

And I don't know why the P.O. Box is the last straw. My nose starts to itch, and then my cell phone makes that doomy sound to indicate it's about to die. My eyes water.

"Everybody has one," Jeff continues from overhead. "You don't have to pay for it or anything."

He hops down through the ceiling just as I'm tucking my dead phone into a desk drawer.

"Is...is something wrong?" he asks.

I sniff and shake my head. Jeff kneels to pet Toothless, but he's looking like he might bolt at any moment. And I don't really blame him; I turn alarmingly red at the first sign of tears. My eyes start watering again, worse this time. I have congenitally stupid tear ducts.

"Oh." Jeff looks at Toothless, then back at me, fishing his phone out of his pocket. "It's okay. I'll text Lisa. Lisa will, um..."

I sob. I can't stop it.

"Just give me a minute," he begs.

He starts to text as I wipe at my face with my sleeve. "You don't need a P.O. Box," he says. "I was just...I thought you might want one. But, uh...don't worry about it?"

Toothless walks over and sets a paw across my legs as I slide down to the floor, and I wrap my arms around his head. Then it all comes out, to the Neanderthal who's pressed up against the far wall looking at me like I might at any moment spew some sort of demonic roundworms from my ears.

"They're going to find...not find..." I wipe my face. Toothless laps at my chin.

Jeff reaches out in front of him like he's patting my shoulder even though he's several feet away. He must really think I have roundworms.

I can't stop the tears as I try to explain, as succinctly as possible and in a way a Neanderthal might actually understand, why Toothless's head not being in the lab is a problem for my veterinary license, and for Toothless should they find him here, and why I already know I can't keep him in a tiny loft apartment. He deserves a big area to run around and someone to drool on all day and no stairs. He's so bad at walking down stairs.

Jeff stands there inertly as I finish, then steps forward and puts a hand out to Toothless. "It'll be okay," he tells me, then, "I promise, Toothless'll be fine."

A snot bubble erupts from one of my nostrils.

"And, uh, you, too," he adds.

I try to suck in deeper breaths, but I'm shaking too hard, and I'm starting to sound like a dementor.

Jeff stays for several minutes, until my breathing's slightly less ominous and Toothless is nearly asleep. Then he promises me sticky buns and a visit from Lisa, who apparently is also magic and should be able to change everything about this situation with just a coat of fresh paint and a little furniture shuffling.

I nod, offering a shaky apology for my outburst and promising to go to Adam's when I'm ready, or at least when I'm a little less red, and Jeff heads off to go hunt down Faye. On a positive note, I guess, at least he's not hunting me. By comparison, the authorities don't seem so bad.

Toothless follows me, tail wagging, as I rinse my face with cool water from the bathroom sink and fish my phone out of the desk. I plug it in so it will have power as soon as the building does, which, given the location of Piney Mountain and the accumulation of ice here, will probably be sometime mid-April. Then I change into my fleece-lined onesie and prepare to hunker down for the night.

I think through various options, from changing my name to bleaching Toothless's hair and giving him enough biotin to turn him into a curly-haired, poodle-esque monster to investing in heavy weaponry and joining an anti-government militia.

Nothing seems sufficient until I see the lawyer walk by my front window. I know he's the lawyer right away, because he's the only person I've seen on the mountain who looks cold. He's wearing a black wool coat that's totally unsuited to ice and makes him look almost like a New Yorker.

The street's clear otherwise, the rest of the townsfolk having gone on what I imagine to be some kind of ritualistic sticky bun feeding frenzy at the inn. So I don't think about how I look before I run out onto the sidewalk and call to him.

He turns to face me, and I catch my reflection in the window. But this is important.

"You're the lawyer, right?"

"Uh..." He takes a step back. "I am." He doesn't sound very sure. Just my luck that I should catch a dud lawyer when I really need one.

"Are you busy?" I ask.

He gestures to where Main Street dead ends into the inn and mutters something about the ice storm, like I might not have noticed.

"I need a...consultation," I say.

"Okay."

I step back and open the front door to my office.

"Um...now?"

I nod and ask him to take off his shoes and coat.

5

The week after the ice almost-apocalypse is full of missed calls and strangers dropping by to check on me. I can't get over how quickly the area recovered from the storm; pickup trucks were salting the roads by the early hours of the next morning, and the power was back on much sooner than I'd thought possible. If there ever were any downed branches, they'd disappeared by the time the streets reopened.

My first set of voicemails are from an officer of the court in Brooklyn. They confirm Mr. Dog Fighting Bastard is sick and that the court's ordered the results of Toothless's rabies test to be released. I guess it was too much to hope for that the man my pit bull was too gentle to kill would be stabbed to death in jail before it could matter that he didn't have rabies.

The other messages are from Steven suggesting we get together later this week to discuss the script for the pageant and offering to help me install a mailbox, since apparently news that I'm not participating in the Piney Falls Post Office Box system traveled quickly.

I look at the lights twinkling in my front window. Last time Steven stopped by, I was out buying dog food at a store in Radford, and he left me a giant wooden beagle with a Christmas light collar to put next to the twig tree.

I listen to the message again—Steven's, not the court drone's—and smile as he starts on the Toothless situation.

Steven discovered my big, drooly secret from Adam, the innkeeper, and has since contacted his MD-ly buddies who work with the court system to see if they can get the rabies concern nixed before further investigation can be made into Toothless's missing head. He says a rabies diagnosis could have been confirmed at least a week ago, anyway. Of course, this would be much easier and less messy with the *victim's* autopsy, but unfortunately, Steven's friends are with the CDC, not the mafia.

The lawyer and I were forced to sneak Toothless into a little storeroom at the inn the night of the ice storm, where Toothless annihilated Adam's remaining supply of sticky bun dough in the time it took me to use the restroom.

By that time, the rest of the town was so interested in Lisa locking the lawyer in a freezer that they didn't even notice the pit bull being led past the dining room. That's something else unexpected about this town—you don't want to piss it off, or you might end up locked in a meat freezer. One minute, Kurt was consulting on a fugitive dog, and the next, an angry interior designer was turning him into a lawyersicle.

Jeff comes through the front door, and I let Toothless greet him with ample drool. But Jeff isn't looking as happy.

"I'm not singing," he tells me before I can ask him what's wrong.

I take a seat on the bench. I get the feeling I should be sitting for this conversation. "Okay," I say, because he seems to be waiting for me to say something.

"As Jesus," he prompts.

"*Jesus?*"

"In the pageant."

I remember Beatrice saying the play had already been cast. "You're...*Jesus?*"

He makes a kind of primitive grunt.

"Really?" Were there no other men on the mountain available to play the savior of mankind, I wonder, or even well-behaved dogs?

"Every year I'm home since I was seventeen," Jeff tells me. His face doesn't change.

"Oh." *Jeff*, as Jesus.

"So no singing," he tells me. "I'm not good, and I don't

like it."

I agree to this, because I don't know what else I could possibly do, and he nods, indicating the conversation's over.

"I have a couple reindeer in my car," he says. "For your roof. A red one and a white one."

"Oh."

"You think both?"

"Both?"

"Lisa said you might have a color...some colors picked out already."

As I mumble something about not having my heart set on any particular color scheme for my rooftop this holiday season, Jeff digs something out of his pocket and extends it towards me.

"And she said to give you this."

I examine the dark bottle. The label says it's melatonin, but I'm a little worried it might be laced with some kind of poison. The last time I saw Lisa, she was with the elusive Faye, and they were glaring at me when they stopped by and saw the lawyer here. I must have been tainted by association.

"It's to sleep," Jeff tells me.

"To sleep?"

"Because you can't sleep. It makes you sleep."

"Oh." I decide not to ask how Lisa knew I've been

having trouble sleeping.

"She got it from her sister, Lauren. She's a nutritionist. And she—Lisa—and Kurt are together now," he adds.

"The lawyer?"

"He's not Heslein's lawyer anymore. That's over. It's okay." He pauses, looking down at Toothless, and then smiles. "Faye was right."

"Great," I say, because I'm not really sure what else to say.

Jeff nods, but he doesn't move.

I try to swallow, but something sticks in my throat. "Is there...anything else I need to know?"

When he meets my eyes, I wish this were just about recasting Jesus.

"Yeah," he says. "I want the dog."

6

The next Tuesday, I'm standing under a gargantuan evergreen decorated with brightly-colored ribbons and Noble Roman's lamps that hover sporadically between its branches like stained glass UFO's. If I were anywhere but Piney Mountain, I'd think the melatonin Lisa's sister sent me was laced with some kind of hallucinogen.

I scan the crowd for Jeff, who promised to bring Toothless with him tonight. As hard as it was for me to part with him, I at least slept a little better over the weekend knowing that any law enforcement officer who might be out after Toothless's still living brain will have to get past the Jeff first. I think the melatonin's helping, too, and Jeff promised Lisa's much happier with me now that she knows I'm not after her lawyer, like anyone in their right mind would be after a lawyer to do anything unlawyerly with.

I spot Faye being dragged through a group of kids and reach her just before Toothless can overturn the hot apple cider booth. Faye wraps her arms around his neck, and he laps at her face. She introduces herself properly for the first time before I can inquire about Toothless's cider intake so far tonight.

"He's the best dog," she says, about "Tuffy."

I bend to scratch Toothless's big, floppy ears. He drools into the front of my coat, and his breath smells like bacon, but he seems well and happy otherwise. *Tuffy*. Really.

She tells me about the special star on the tree then, and about the spot in the preserve where it will be replanted after Christmas.

When it's time to start the ceremony, Jeff agrees to leave Toothless with me and gently nudges Faye towards the microphone. She seems reluctant at first, but the crowd hushes when she steps up to the platform. Toothless lies down at my feet and watches reverently as she begins an old poem about Piney Mountain. It's the kind of poem where 'snow' rhymes with 'no,' with 'glistens' and 'listens' and 'mittens' galore, but there's something about it goes right through me.

Adam hands me a tapered candle when Faye lights a

larger one up on the platform and starts to pass the flame through the crowd. The old-fashioned Christmas lights swinging over the streets of the town square are shut off then, and it's quiet enough to hear little gusts of wind rushing between the buildings as the candles are lit. I notice a group of musicians decked out in red, green, and blue on a larger platform at the side of the tree. The lamps on their music stands glow in a hazy little circle until my eyes adjust to the darkness and I can make out some of the faces in the crowd.

I get the flame from Adam and pass it to a surprisingly still little boy sitting on Toothless's hip. Once all the candles are lit, Jeff steps up to the microphone and says a prayer. It sounds foreign, incantations interspersed with words I don't recognize that must be in some language as old as the mountain itself. He raises his candle at the end, and the musicians begin a soft rendition of "Silent Night" that seems to be carried away from us with the wind.

As I watch the boy next to me staring, wide-eyed, at the dark tree, I get the feeling I've walked into some intensely personal experience, the kind of holiday ritual that means something much more to the people who call this place home. It almost makes me wish I had a tradition like this, something beyond Cracker Barrel. Maybe I've been missing out on more than I thought all these years of treeless Christmases in impersonal cities.

My breath clouds in front of my face, and silence falls again as the song ends. Then, suddenly, the tree bursts to life with a blinding flash of light. The crowd cheers as the orchestra segues into "Sleigh Ride," and I get the feeling I'm looking at the tree in the same state of awe as they are, in all its beribboned, Noble Roman's glory. Jeff slides his arm around Faye, and several couples in the crowd kiss. It's like a living compilation of all the romanticism of a Norman Rockwell Christmas painting, but with pizza lamps.

"What do you think of the tree?"

I jump as Beatrice appears at my side. She's wearing a long burgundy dress and a white puff coat with golden scarves wrapped around her ears. I can't tell where she came from; the group of teenagers who were behind me before have run off.

I pause in the middle of a question about the significance of all the blue ribbons when I realize Adam's frowning at the witch.

"You said you wouldn't be here," he says.

Beatrice waves a scarf. "How funny," she says. "I must have gotten the date wrong." Then she turns to me. "Steven's at his conference, you know. He'd be here otherwise."

I think I actually flush at 'Steven.' I reach down to pet Toothless. He licks my mitten before turning and lapping up the little boy's drink when he's facing the other way. It's a good thing he's such a big dog and doesn't seem to be very sensitive to cider. Or to pizza, lasagna, cookies, or socks.

When Jeff and Faye get back to us, Jeff tugs the leash away from me as I'm trying to congratulate them on the service—I think it was a service, anyway, of some kind—and my cell phone rings in my pocket. It takes me a second to recognize Steven's number. Beatrice winks at me as I excuse myself and walk to a quieter spot.

On the phone, Steven sounds unusually full of cheer for someone at a cardiology conference. He greets me with good tidings of a happy tree lighting and inquires about Toothless, my new rooftop reindeer, and the tree.

I stare off into the crowd as our conversation segues into the special paper mache star. The music wafts this way, and I can see steam rising off the Noble Roman's lamps and floating away into the darkness.

I move aside to avoid being trampled by some laughing kids running back towards the square as Steven fills me in on the after-lighting sledding and more potent cider traditions at Jeff's place.

"But don't worry," he adds. "They'll have a snowsuit for you."

I have a brief flash of trying to shove my newly sticky bun-laden thighs into a snowsuit and decide to change the subject, asking him how his conference is going.

"Oh, you know, nothing exciting," he says. "I'll be

back Thursday and should be able to get up the mountain by that evening. I was wondering if you might want to get together then. Maybe we could get dinner?"

"Thursday's..." My stomach says *entirely unacceptable,* and my brain repeats its *No eating with handsome, potentially normal mountainfolk* spiel, but something that sounds suspiciously like a middle school-aged girl squeaks "perfect," instead.

"Great," Steven says. "Can I pick you up around six?"

"We could meet at Cracker Barrel," I suggest. And there's my instinct seeking country-style comfort in a strange land. I step closer to the post office to block the wind.

"Cracker Barrel?" Steven asks after a couple seconds.

"There's one in Radford," I tell him. "It's close to you, isn't it?"

"Oh, no, it's okay," he says. "I don't mind driving up."

I shake my head. This is one of those times I know I'll need the familiar support of Cracker Barrel; it's been eons since I've been on anything even resembling a date.

"I won't be driving that long once I catch my flight back, and..."

"I've been wanting to go," I tell him.

"Oh," he says, then, "To Radford?"

My reflection bobs up and down in the window of the post office, a smile there that looks like a housecat who's just eaten a complete gerbil. "To Cracker Barrel," I say.

7

On Thursday, everything in the Radford Cracker Barrel's as it should be—the rocking chairs and the fireplace and the giant checkerboard, the bright wall of candy and all the old posters in the dining area. It smells like freshly baked biscuits and home. There's no indication this one's any different, that it's anywhere near Piney Mountain.

I take a breath as I finish the triangle peg game and roll up the sleeves of my sweater where they're bunching over my wrists. The game wasn't as easy as usual with Steven watching from across the table.

He tells me he's impressed. I can always leave just one peg, and I want to preen, but the truth is that I've had a lot of practice. Everywhere I moved with my parents while they were being transferred to different military centers, there was always a Cracker Barrel near a highway to serve as a kind of home base.

I try to explain this to Steven in a way that doesn't make me sound like a gypsy, but he's looking at me with sympathy when I finish. His expression doesn't change when I tell him about how amazing the Coca Cola cake is at every Cracker Barrel and about the checkers tournaments I used to have with my dad on the front porches on long summer evenings and how I've collected all the state refrigerator magnets.

"You never stayed anywhere more than a couple years?" he asks.

I shake my head. But that's the thing about Cracker Barrels—there are rocking chairs on every front porch, homemade biscuits and fresh preserves or corn bread. It's hard to miss anything when you move from one to the next.

Steven looks skeptical but, after some prodding about his own childhood, he concedes things might have been a little easier for him if he'd moved around more. The name and reputation of his great-aunt still haunt him in Radford, where she gets her nails done. He explains how, since her husband's death, Lucy Lowens has expanded her streak of terror to even younger victims, barking orders during preschool performances and making the marching band members cry during some kind of wooly bear parade in March. He's started handing out candy at the bottom of her driveway on Halloween, he says, since she refuses to participate in the Piney Falls trick-or-treating traditions.

I drink some sweet tea and request more Lucy Lowens stories, which all make her sound like a fairy tale villain. But even when he's talking about his inhumanly evil great aunt, there's something kind and easy about Steven that makes me feel like he belongs in a Cracker Barrel.

We talk for a bit about difficult patients, both human and hairy, and about how we found our careers. He wanted to be a vet once.

"Until a goat peed on me in a third grade production of the nativity," he tells me.

I inhale some sweet tea as he describes the scene.

"What about you?" he asks. "When did you know?"

"Visiting 4-H bunnies during a heat wave in Louisiana." I was eight, and my parents helped me get a bunch of fans to put on the rabbits after we read in the paper that a couple of them had died of heat exhaustion. It was the right start to a career in animal loving for someone who couldn't keep a pet. I tell Steven about all the 4-H fairs my parents took me to in different states and how sad I always was when the animals went back to their homes.

The waitress stops by to take our orders, and I ask for my traditional eggs in the basket. Steven promises to try my Coca Cola cake.

"You're a vegetarian," he says when the waitress

walks away.

It's something easy enough to be New York, where no one knows you, but I've always kept it a secret when we lived on military bases in smaller towns lest I be burned at the stake as some sort of meatless witch. Though I guess this town reveres its witches.

I nod and wait for Steven's face to change, for some suspicion to show there. It doesn't come. Instead, he tells me about recent research on animal proteins that suggests they're a common contributor to inflammation.

The food comes quickly like always, but it's one of those dinners that lasts longer than dessert and a second sweet tea, the kind meant for extra scoops of vanilla bean ice cream and slow browsing in the country store before the restaurant closes for the night.

By the time we're having dessert, the candle on the table's running low on oil, and they've turned down the lights as the general hustle and bustle of Radford—that's what it's called here when people go home to catch the late *Jeopardy* show before the QVC Christmas shopping specials start up—dies down and we're left in the dining room alone.

We talk about heartworms and favorite books then, bad Christmas gifts and trans fats. Steven asks if I have special plans for the holidays this year, and not about all the ones I spent as a child, like most people do, curious about kids who didn't have a childhood like theirs. And I feel the way I always do here, my belly full of Cola cake and sweet tea as this time with him joins all my other happy Cracker Barrel memories.

8

The magic spell of Cracker Barrel lasted right up until Steven brought me home. After all my worries about the Neanderthal crushing me when he dropped down from a ceiling tile, I can't believe it was the door-that-stuck that finally got me and sent me tumbling back into Main Street.

I'm lying on Steven's ankle now. His slacks smell like fresh preserves and cornbread.

"Are you okay?" His shoulders are blocking my view of the awning over my door, and I realize his hand's around the back of my neck.

He shines his phone's flashlight into my eyes. "Did you lose consciousness?" he asks.

"Hmm mmm." I sit up, and the room spins. Only I'm

not in a room. It's the street spinning. "Maybe a little," I say.

I reach up to touch the back of my head. "Your ankle..." I look over at his elbow. It's his arm I'm lying on. And I'm almost sure I fell on his ankle.

He's frowning at me. "Do you remember what happened?" he asks.

"My door," I tell him. "It sticks." It started after the ice storm. I was meaning to get it fixed. Or, you know, just take it off, since about anyone willing to climb the mountain already has a key. And if for some reason they don't, they can just come in through my ceiling.

I sit up, and Steven puts a hand on my elbow.

"Wait just a minute, okay?" He pulls at the door, which opens smoothly for him, of course. Then he props it open with his foot and helps me stand.

Steven's arm's around my back when we walk inside, and I get another waft of him, biscuits and Cola cake this time.

"Do you feel like you're going to vomit?"

So much for that. I shake my head just as my stomach lurches. Steven tries to guide me toward the couch as I feel the Cola cake start to make its way back up my esophagus.

I make a break for the bathroom and almost lose the Cola cake to the toilet. Steven's right behind me when I straighten and look up in the mirror, and I splash some water on my face. My stomach gurgles as he guides me over to sit on the toilet lid before I can muster a reasonable protest.

"There's just a little blood," he says, placing a hand on my shoulder like you might a cat getting ready to jump out a window. He uses his other hand to wring out a washcloth.

I'm pretty sure my face is bright red, any blood aside. And everything was going so smoothly at Cracker Barrel.

My head twinges as Steven gently dabs a washcloth across the back. He doesn't let me take it away from him when I try to express how unnecessary this is—because I do this all the time, at least for dogs. I can see the cloth's bloody when he steps away and rinses it out in the sink.

As Steven's cleaning the wound, he tries to distract me with simple questions about books and TV shows I like. My head stings a little, and I have more trouble answering with him standing so close. So I'm not thinking entirely clearly when I admit I only faithfully watch *Meercat Manor* and that I've missed several episodes since I moved here and don't have service anymore. I don't know any shows that aren't on the animal channels.

Steven rinses out the washcloth one last time and finishes dabbing at my head, and I stand up slowly and study my reflection in the mirror. My head seems to have stopped bleeding, at least.

"I think you did lose consciousness for a second," he

says, stepping around me to examine my pupils again. "But you shouldn't worry. There's a regional hospital in Radford that..."

He pauses when I'm guessing my eyes bulge out like a shih tzu.

"Don't worry," he says. "They have a new open MRI and basic operating room services. They wouldn't have a problem treating a concussion, if..."

I'm shaking my head, and I guess he quits talking to stop me from flinging cerebrospinal fluid all over the bathroom.

I assure him I'm fine and try to make this sound like my professional opinion. Dogs do this all the time, running into doors, and I've never seen any permanent damage. Toothless usually opens doors with his forehead. "Really," I add. I don't even think I'm going to puke anymore.

"Your pupils look even," Steven concedes, stepping back again, "but it wouldn't hurt to stop in at the hospital for a quick scan, and we'll want to keep an eye on you, awake, for the next several hours."

My stomach lurches even more violently at the combination of 'hospital' and 'we.'

"It wouldn't take long," he adds. "I know the ER doctor on call most weekends. He's great."

I shake my head, evidently too violently, and want to

throw up again. "Not necessary. Really, I'm..." I think of bags of fluids, of syringes on those squeaky silver carts, of needles everywhere. "...Totally normal," I finish, standing and walking to the front of the main room.

Steven's at my side to catch my arm as I trip over the same uneven strip of floorboard I always trip over. I really need to let Jeff fix that.

"Thanks," I tell him. "I really appreciate..."

He waves a hand to stop me. "You really should be a little closer to a hospital. Everything looks okay right now, and if you want to wait, not go in unless you get a headache or something changes, I understand."

I shake my head again, and he frowns at me.

"Is there some reason you wouldn't want to go to the hospital? I do think you were out for a few seconds, which wouldn't necessarily be anything to worry about in itself, but falling on the back of your..."

"I have a little...phobia...of hospitals," I admit, which somehow tastes worse coming out of my mouth than I think Cola cake bile would.

Steven looks back and forth between my pupils. "But you're a vet," he says.

"It's, um...I broke my arm when I was seven, and the needles..." I take a steadying breath.

"You're not afraid of needles, surely?"

I fiddle with the top of a *Prevention* magazine on the counter.

"But you give shots," Steven says.

I focus on the magazine. I can remove feet of intestines without a problem, but if one of the vet techs shows me the wrong kind of needle, I have to open a window. I only use the really tiny ones.

I meet Steven's eyes again, and he bites his lip. Now I can't stop looking at his lip.

"Okay," he says, after a few seconds. "So we'll go to my house. It's closer to the hospital, just in case there are any red flags of a concussion later on." He reaches out a hand.

I stare at it. This isn't how a man's supposed to ask you to come to his house, all full of concern and waiting patiently for you to vomit.

"Please," he says. "For my peace of mind."

As I sense the mysterious forces of Piney Falls pushing me to take his hand, I wonder if this is how a concussion feels.

Steven seems to have considered a lot of logistics by the time I agree to go with him. He takes my keys to lock the front door after shutting me in his SUV. Like locking the door could matter. There's not even a pit bull inside to steal anymore.

The drive back to Radford's cool and dark. He uses the time to try to assure me that my needle phobia's totally normal, telling me about one adult patient of his who secretly refuses to swallow even the tiniest of pills.

We turn up a long gravel driveway on the other side of the preserve, and his home comes into view. It's lovely, of course, like he is, a sprawling ranch with stone and wood and big windows set back a little ways from the road just outside the Radford city limits. He makes sure to open his front door before I can get close to it.

An hour and a half later, I'm wearing Steven's socks and am propped up on the chaise portion of a long sofa under a chunky woven blanket. *Meercat Manor's* playing on a big TV in front of me.

He bends over me again with a flashlight to examine my pupils, and this time, my stomach feels warm and tingly in a way that doesn't make me think I'm going to throw up.

He says my pupils look good, which makes me blush. Then he says we should watch at least a couple more episodes of *Meercat Manor* before I go to sleep.

9

This morning, I woke up to the smell of eggs and toast from Steven's guest bed, my stomach full of warm fuzzies and sweet butterflies. But things can turn quickly on this mountain. Eight hours later, I'm wishing I could hide under a church pew, and my stomach's spewing acid.

In just the last half hour, the pomeranian in my lap's been cast as the Christ child, Toothless has dragged a menorah through an Eid al-Fitr feast, and the children's choir has descended on the cookie table behind the altar like a hoard of glitter-covered zombies.

I squeeze the pomeranian. He belongs to Angela, the nice woman from the post office who let us borrow him when Lucy Lowens forbade the use of her newest grandniece as Jesus. Evidently, Steven's aunt has a problem with Faye, who plays Mary, holding the baby, no doubt envisioning some transfer of her psychic powers.

And so Puffy's on my lap now, a little unsure about his new role as the savior of mankind, as the three wise men read through their lines and Steven tries to herd the children, their ringleader brandishing a menorah like a samurai, away from the cookie table. These cookies are labeled as practice cookies for the Bakeoff, experimental in a way I can only assume mixed with Piney Mountain air could turn the children into real samurai.

I take a deep breath as Jeff joins me in the front pew. He's wearing purple crushed velvet bell bottoms and a tye-dyed robe in preparation for the "Jesus Christ, Superstar" number that rather shockingly starts the show. The disco ball overhead later transforms into a giant Star of David.

"Adam was thinking it should swing from the back of the stage," Jeff says.

I agree, because I'm not in a position quibble about the beginning location of the disco ball that foretold the birth of Christ. I'm guessing Beatrice herself directed the pageant sometime in the 70's.

Faye joins us in the pew and inquires about the status of my head bump, which I assume she probably foresaw but failed to warn me about.

"It's better, then?" she asks.

"Much better, thanks."

"And it looks like everything's going really smoothly here," she says, reaching across Jeff to scratch Puffy's head. Behind her, Beatrice abandons her post at the cookie table, which is currently swarmed by fairies. Faye must have a very different idea of what 'smoothly' entails. At least Puffy seems to like her, since she has to birth him in the second act.

Beatrice rubs her hands together, looking like a cross between Dr. Evil and Mrs. Claus as she approaches.

"You look marvelous," she tells me. "You're *glowing*, and this is all just perfect."

I try to thank her, but I'm not sure what 'perfect' means to her. Probably something like 'smoothly' means to her grand-niece.

After a few minutes of script discussions, Beatrice excuses herself to attempt to herd the fairies, and Puffy works up enough courage to hop off my lap and follow her through the throng of children.

"You and Steven must be having a lot of fun with this," Faye says to me. She looks serious. Maybe she has a different idea of what 'fun' means, too.

"Oh," I say, "It's...fun." But my mind's still on eggs and toast and sweet, milky drinks from Steven's espresso maker this morning. I squint at the backstage area, where he's trying to count the little angels.

"Have you met Lucy?" Faye asks.

I shake my head, and I swear I can feel something rattling around in the back of my skull.

"That's okay," Faye says. "She lost her husband a few

years ago around Christmas, and she's really more her best in the summertime."

Of course. She's like the tomatoes, I guess. My only information on Lucy Lowens, other than Steven's portrayal of her as Cruella DeVille, is that she doesn't want Faye to touch her newest family member, so I find Faye an unlikely defender of the grand-Grinch.

"Steven's nothing like her," she tells me.

I try to agree casually, but warmth prickles over my chest.

When Jeff and Faye take their places for the first number, Steven leaves the children to Beatrice's care and takes the space beside me for the beginning of the runthrough. Being able to smell him again, my mind drifts to steaming coffees in the snow and summer nights of Cola cake. It's probably my head injury, I tell myself, and something that will one day be widely recognized as "sticky bun brain."

He leans closer to show me the additions in the script requested by the wise men, which now include a woman, and compliments me on my handling of the fairy wing crisis. Despite the pieces of fairy wing that might now be a permanent addition to my sweater, I know duct taping was the easy director's job, though; I didn't have to handle Lucy Lowens on the phone. Steven was at least able to keep her away from the rehearsals. He said it was in the interest of not frightening the children, but I suspect his quick thinking saved me some terror, too.

We turn back to the stage as the music starts. I'd never have expected Jeff to be so comfortable in his role as Jesus, but he slides across the floor triumphantly on the first chords of "Jesus Christ, Superstar." Then the wise men march majestically to the Eid feast, and the kindergarten presents take extra bows after their song. Even the disco ball swoops gracefully across the stage, and I have to admit I feel a bit of awe when it sheds its outer layer and turns in to the Star of David.

Maybe most astonishingly, Beatrice makes a convincing angel. Her voice shakes the organ pipes in the back of the church.

"She was an opera singer," Steven whispers to me as she finishes the unaccompanied "Oh, Holy Night" from the balcony before the little angels join in with their "Gloria" as they dance their way up to the manger.

Puffy clings to Faye's sweater when she tries to lift him to the wise men, but even a pomeranian Christ child doesn't take away from the conglomerate magic of so many years of trippy script changes. And there's something so lovely about the madness, a character all of its own that makes the mountain vibrate with holiday spirit. Even the littlest Eid presents in the audience are quiet until everyone joins in on the "Joy to the World" finale, which I'm pretty sure can be heard all the way down Main Street at the inn.

Steven and points to the stage, indicating our bow location, and then, afterwards, he stays with me to greet the throng of duct-taped fairies and angels as they come by with their parents to say hello.

Once I've met every last parent, Bakeoff entrant, and member of the Piney Falls knitting club and think I'm going to collapse, he steers me to a futon backstage and hands over a steaming thermos of cider.

"Jeff's been working on it," he tells me. "It's a family recipe."

I thank him, and we talk about Christmas and the community for a while, sipping cider in the quiet narthex as the church clears out. He assures me everything's in order with the sound system and the spotlight for the dress rehearsal on Saturday, and I can't help but feel a little *ping* of excitement deep in my belly. It's something about the mountain air, I think. Or the sticky buns, or the cider. Or him. It's so easy to get swept away here.

We're getting ready to go to Adam's for the first in an informal series of community holiday dinners when there's more noise from the sanctuary and Adam himself meets us backstage with a box of sticky buns he's clutching to his chest.

Steven stands, and I drink the last of my cider and turn away to sweep up some glitter. I hope there isn't any threat of another sticky bun shortage.

"He's, uh, kinda insistent about seeing her," Adam says, his eyes moving past Steven and settling on me.

And I don't know if it's Adam's face or a cue from whatever worms are living in my intestines that now's the time to flee, or something I've really known for weeks, but suddenly, I want to violently expel the cider.

Steven walks in front of me, and we peek through the curtain. Beatrice is conversing with a man in a long, dark coat in the center aisle.

I hope beyond reason that he's some nasty ex-boyfriend come to rob me or kill me or just be a pain in my butt for the rest of my mortal existence. But I know he's something worse, because I don't have any ex-boyfriends I'd be willing to give up my already-consumed cider and a festive dinner with Steven to avoid. I don't have many ex-boyfriends to begin with.

Beatrice is close behind the intruder when he reaches the stairs of the apse and extends his hand, clearly recognizing me as the only dog-napper and illegal-doer on the mountain.

"Dr. Norton?" he asks. "Annie Norton?"

I nod, but my hand doesn't move to take his. He shows his ID, telling me he's from a court in Radford, and starts to explain about Toothless's owner being sick. But of course, they can't find Toothless's head to test his brain for Rabies or anything else. This is all just as expected, of course, right on cue.

"I'll need to ask you some questions about the dog," he finishes. His chest is puffed out in self-importance, and he brandishes his identification with all the brazenness of a mall cop catching a group of college kids smoking weed in a parking lot. I don't realize I'm holding my breath until Beatrice speaks.

"But it's *dinnertime*, Officer Olsten," she says. "As I was saying, you can't deprive our veterinarian of dinner."

"It won't take…"

"We're *all* going to dinner."

I look over, and Steven and Adam both nod obediently.

"The whole town," Beatrice adds. "It's a tradition."

Bill Olsten, acting as agent of an out-of-state court and almost certainly on the biggest job of his career with the Radford police department, starts to flush. When he says he's not hungry, Beatrice shoves a cookie into his hand.

"That's Lucy Lowens' lady fingers," she tells him. "They took second place last year."

Olsten murmurs incoherently, and his cheeks redden even more as he stares down at the lady finger.

Beatrice turns away. "Now, Adam, do we have sticky buns?"

"Yes, ma'am."

"Good," she says. Then she loops an arm through Olsten's elbow and marches him out of the sanctuary.

10

I don't call my parents until the next day, when I'm wishing I'd accepted Adam's offer to take home a box of sticky buns.

My dad sounds like he did when I announced I was getting my first menstrual period on a two week trip to Uruguay.

"And you told this man that you left the dog's head with the lab?" he asks.

"Right." I think my hope was that, if I told people, it would be accepted as truth by default, like that your hamster needs a rabies shot or that declawing cats is okay. Which of course I'd never even consider telling anyone. So I was pretty out of practice at lying.

Of all the bad I envisioned coming from lying to a

court, though, I wasn't counting on the bastard whose actions sent Toothless into my care in the first place getting some sort of mystery illness after he was taken into custody. Not that foresight would have changed my mind or anything; I've gone sort of illogical and legally reckless lately.

"But they can't find the head?" my mom asks, shouting into the speakerphone. My dad might panic at a little period blood, but my mom's made of tougher stuff. Had she been in my situation, she probably would have thought to cut off the head of some other, already dead dog.

"They checked each head in the lab," I say. "None were for a pit bull matching Toothless's description." I remember how Olsten told me this with a frown, reading it off the papers he'd been given on the case like there must be some sort of pit bull headnapping scheme afoot. He probably thinks I'm the thief and have a rotting dog head somewhere in my belongings that he'll find as soon as he can get a warrant.

I can hear my voice is shaking like it never does on the phone with my parents, and they quickly switch topics and try to distract me with tales of creepy Italian Christmas dolls and strange delicacies from the islands.

"I said I had no idea why the head was missing," I say when my mom, forgetting the topic change, asks for clarification about my illegal declarations to this point.

It was Jeff who suggested the presence of the head thief, actually. And when Jeff joined in the conversation at the inn last night, Officer Olsten suddenly realized it was getting late and hurried out the door with a vague threat he'd return after he'd looked into everything.

"And this is all because of the guy in jail?" Dad asks.

"Right. He's still sick." Since he was bitten by Toothless, they've started the shots for rabies, anyway, so I don't know why it matters if it's rabies or something else they probably couldn't get from his head, anyway. I told Olsten I couldn't precisely remember the date I received Toothless at the vet clinic, since animal control doesn't keep very good records of transfers. And of course I couldn't just present him with the perfectly healthy dog I was court-ordered to euthanize and claim to have beheaded.

"And he's a what?" My dad means the man who got Toothless into my care to begin with.

"A teacher." Which caused the court, in all its stupidity, to dissemble. It makes the system want to save him a little more, being a *teacher* who beat his son and was gearing up to fight his dog. If the guy would have hit a cop instead of a child, they'd probably have shot him and been done with it.

"Oh, honey," Mom says.

"Isn't there something they can do with the kid's

bruises?" Dad asks.

"No." The guy's still being paid by the school until the case is resolved, on some sort of indefinite leave. The state's even paying to keep him in a hospital for a little fever, where he's probably at this moment eating sherbet and watching soaps.

I fiddle with my triangle peg game and try to stay calm through the rest of the conversation with my parents, who want to know more about Piney Falls. It's hard to describe, but I tell them about the excess of cold and trees and community here. It felt like the whole town was gathered around our table at some point last night, alternately feeding Olsten Bakeoff cookies and looking at him like they were personally going to cook him for Christmas dinner.

Jeff had Toothless spirited away to his cabin before he joined us at the inn, so I at least know he's safe. I wouldn't pass Jeff, especially on his own turf, to get to a dragon carrying bird flu and tapeworm larvae and firing them out all over Virginia. But even he can't save my license for violating a direct court order.

I ignore a knock at the front door that's probably Steven checking on me, since he's the only mountain dweller who knocks, and start to cry.

The storeroom looks barren with its bunch of unpacked boxes, and I look around at all the nic nacs I've already taken out that I'm going to have to stuff back into my car. It's only a matter of time before the court will be able to prove I didn't send Toothless's head to the lab. Then it will only be a matter of time after that before they'll ask for witnesses to the euthanasia, and the vet techs will all confirm I did this at night, after everyone else had gone home. Crooked vets can kill or maim every species known to man with unnecessary procedures, but one sweet pit bull who one judge thought should be dead is enough to sink an otherwise uneventful career. Even if they let me off with just a fine and a suspension, I won't be able to afford my own office.

My parents can hear all this in my voice. Dad asks about the town's Christmas traditions, probably thinking this will cheer me up, and I try to focus on describing the giant living tree with the Noble Roman's lamps.

It shouldn't be what gets me, but I feel the tears coming anyway. Before Piney Falls, holidays were always fine for me, usually by myself in emergency clinics treating dogs who'd gotten into fondue pots. I've always been happy with leftover Cracker Barrel, the company of the soothing narrators on Animal Planet, and the high drama of *Meercat Manor*.

But this Christmas was going to be different. I was even starting to be able to sleep here. I don't think it's the melatonin Lisa gave me, either. It was like everything was starting to be different right up until Olsten showed up in the church.

My mom tells me about singing a particularly rough version of "Oh, Holy Night!" in a show for the kids on base, and I decide to wait to tell them about my plans to abscond my new mountain, this time with no dog in tow. I should get away now, I know—even with a license suspension, I could be assisting someone as a tech in one of the cities by the new year, vaccinating Christmas puppies and helping spay cats by springtime.

But I want to be part of a Piney Falls holiday, just this once. I think of Steven again, of the parties he's told me about at Jeff's tree farm and late nights at the inn and Christmas mornings in the snow.

I'll still be thinking about him long after I've driven away. The pageant's on the 23rd, so I make a quick plan to leave the next morning, Christmas Eve. That should give Gliel enough time to rent the building for January.

I run myself a bath as I'm wishing my parents a happy Christmas, which they'll spend on a friend's sailboat around the Grecian islands. I turn up the temperature of the water and let it fill the bathroom with steam. I'll have to face the town at the dress rehearsal tomorrow and want to make sure my face redness has gone down at least a little by then. My eyes would probably scare the little fairies if they could see me now.

"You're going to be all right," Mom promises before I hang up. "It's almost Christmas."

I say something reassuring, but even an hour long

bath can't take the redness out of my eyes.

11

Nothing goes as planned at the dress rehearsal. Before we even get started, major characters have been recast, a fairy's needed stitches after punching a fist through a stained glass window (samurai fighting), and our new Mary looks about as likely to murder Joseph as to birth the Christ pomeranian.

Beatrice assures me this is a long-held tradition on Piney Mountain, everything going wrong at the dress rehearsal. Actually, Beatrice *types* to me that this is all normal and that everything will turn out all right. She's smiling when she hands me the ipad, like her visions might somehow bring comfort to me now. I guess she hasn't foreseen me running away the morning after the show.

I try not to think about the paperwork I'll need to do

to get out of the lease or about finding a new place to stay as Adam wrestles with the star/disco ball a few rows ahead of mine. I thought my concerns this week would all be on the likely loss of my license, not on the loss of the town, but the town seems to be winning out right now. And Steven's another thing altogether.

He's helping Faye, who appears to be on the verge of a complete witchy meltdown as he secures the angel wings to her robe. Our previous Mary, Faye hasn't looked very angelic since Beatrice waltzed in and announced in an ominous whisper that she'll be losing her voice and so won't be able to sing the angel's part.

As Faye's pulling at her wings and presumably looking for something on which to break her vocal box, her replacement's pacing around the manger like a sweatered rhino stampeding the carpeted savannah. Mary is now being played by Lisa's sister, Lauren, who arrived in town somewhat unexpectedly and obviously wants to be anywhere but Piney Mountain for the holidays.

Beatrice assured me Lauren's present state has more to do with being trapped at the inn with Adam than with her new role, but this seems unlikely; sticky buns are unlimited to guests, and Adam's pretty likable. I don't want to judge her too harshly, though, since she's responsible for my melatonin.

Beatrice walks away, rhinestoned ipad waving, to herd the children backstage, and Toothless chews on some leftover tulle beside me. With Olsten safely back in Radford, Jeff was able to bring him tonight to provide emotional support for me, since everyone seems to think I'm suffering from some sort of directors' stage fright.

Tuffy, as Jeff insists on calling him, is particularly fond of the chewable fairies' uniforms, and the children seem equally delighted with him. It helps to ease the sting of leaving him a little. It's always hard to give up an animal, even to the best of homes, but at least I feel confident my sweet, defenseless pit bull will have an army of little fairies and Jeff to defend him should he ever be identified by the court system.

Toothless, tail wagging, trots backstage, and I notice Jeff holding Faye back by the wings as Beatrice passes by with a plate of Bakeoff preview cookies to bribe the children. Steven slides into the pew beside me, and we're pushed together by the wise men and woman as they seek sanctuary from all the kids backstage. I take a deep breath as the lights dim.

Then that old adage about everything going wrong at once proves true. Jeff trips over a speaker cord and crashes into the Eid presents, and then Adam, whose guidance of the disco ball across the stage usually borders on *Phantom of the Opera*-quality, lets loose of the rope midway through its trek over the altar. It bounces and rolls down the center aisle like a big, sparkly bowling ball.

"Don't worry," Steven tells me as the wise men leap

into action to reassemble it. "Something like this happens every year at the dress rehearsal. I think it's a curse. Joseph got the flu last year, and the year before, the baby Jesus vomited all over the stable."

As we sit here with Beatrice silently ordering more duct tape for the disco ball, I don't think about the Christ child puking or even about the possibility of an errant disco ball dropping on an audience member. Probably because I'm thinking about my knee brushing against Steven's in the pew and indulging some misguided fantasy about late night *Meercat Manor* and Cracker Barrel rocking chairs and shared Coca Cola cake.

Maybe I'll catch some eggs in the basket on my way out of Virginia. I promised myself this morning that I won't regret this holiday, at least, that I'll do everything I can to enjoy my last couple nights on the mountain. Maybe I'll even keep a little Christmas tradition that will stick with me wherever I am next year. If nothing else, Piney Mountain's convinced me it's time to develop some holiday traditions of my own.

A few minutes later, the flying disco ball's been repaired and looks none the worse for wear, and the fairies have all been herded backstage and pacified by more cookies.

A hush falls when the runthrough resumes, and Faye stomps out to the mic like an angel of vengeance, glaring at Beatrice as her new piano accompaniment begins.

"She'll be okay with this tomorrow," Steven whispers. "Really, you know, she should have seen it coming."

I smile, because he's smiling, and because I can't help it. I can honestly say Faye's is the most unique rendering of "Oh, Holy Night!" I've ever heard, violent in a way that makes you scared for the high note. It stays pretty terrifying all the way through, but when it's finished, I notice Beatrice is grinning.

The angels are joined for their number by Toothless, who's now wearing a tutu. Then the Eid feast is interrupted by Puffy's yelp from backstage, but my eyes are watering a little even before the birth of the Christ pomeranian.

Adam, as Joseph, paces like a real, clueless new father as the Star of David sways gently above them. I blot at my eyes when the fairies are thanking the moon and the stars and everything bright and beautiful for this perfect night, because there's something eerily powerful about a Piney Mountain holiday in all its nuttery that I know I'll remember forever.

Afterwards, a triumphant cast gathers in the aisle, and Beatrice leads the group out the back doors to a celebratory dinner at the inn.

I retreat to the backstage area as they're leaving, little angels and fairies snagging ziplocks of Bakeoff cookies before their parents can coax them home to bed.

There's a trail of glitter through the wings with stray ribbons and bits of duct tape stuck to the carpet. I pick up a few pieces before unplugging the trees at the sides of the stage and turning off the lights in the bathroom.

Steven's there when I step back into the wings.

"Ready?" he asks.

I nod, and he helps me into my coat, slinging my bag over his shoulder as we walk out of the church together. We talk about the wise men's carols and the fairy dance until we get to the parking lot. He takes my arm to help me over an icy spot, and we pause a few steps from my car.

"I was going to go back to Lucy's on Christmas Eve. Because she's alone otherwise," he says. He always makes the witch hat with his hands when he describes his aunt's solitary holiday traditions or jokes about her cooking children in her oven. "I was wondering, if you don't have plans yet, if you might..." He looks down, then back at me. "I was hoping you might come with me."

I open my mouth. Every fiber of my being wants to scream *yes!*—loudly, to everything and to anyone who will listen. Except that sad part of my tired gypsy core that knows I can't. I'll be off the mountain long before Christmas Eve dinner. But it punches me in the stomach when I finally spit it out.

"I'm sorry," I tell him. "I can't."

12

All the melatonin in Virginia couldn't put me to sleep after the dress rehearsal. I've re-packed all my boxes and loaded them into my car by four the next morning. This way, I can leave right after the pageant and drive through the night. I'll go to Ohio first, to a weekly rental hotel in the middle of nowhere where I can regroup and put together applications for vet clinics in some cities. It's really all I can do until I know what's happening with my license.

They won't be anything like this place, of course, but I'll stay busy, like I always do, and hopefully, I'll be settled somewhere new before I've had a chance to think too much about everything I've driven away from here.

By six, I've sent the necessary emails to the town's now ex-mayor Gliel and the bank.

So, by six-thirty, the only place I have left to go is the church. People won't start arriving for the pageant for several more hours, and I'm grateful to have a plentiful supply of Amy's veggie lasagnas and Bakeoff cookies to hold me over until then.

When I get inside, I dump the food in the communal freezer and keep myself busy for a while picking duct tape out of the carpet, ironing angels' robes, and dusting the pews with some natural lemony cleaner I found under the sink in the bathroom.

While I work, I tell myself this is how it's supposed to be. I go over every reason I can think of why Piney Falls is the wrong place for my practice—like that it has a climate that could make even sled dogs uncomfortable and is the kind of place where cats are picked up by bigger cats, dogs are eaten by bears, bunnies get frostbite on their little toes, and hamsters probably go missing in the snow. Their owners should be more volatile than in other places I've practiced, too. SAD breeds suicides in climates like these, people OD on cough medicines and aren't found for days, or they flip over their cars on icy back roads and are eaten by bears or stay perfectly preserved hunks of frozen humans at the bottoms of rivers after falling through the ice on rare sunny days. Not to mention all the arthritis and fibromyalgia. Really, I tell myself, it's a wonder I've made it this long. I expected to see inflammation in most of my joints by now, given the altitude and the cold and everything else, but the only noticeable signs of swelling in my body now are around my eyes.

I finish dusting the pews as I'm trying to remember how many minutes of ice-walking can cause nerve damage to a dog's paws. But later, while I'm wondering about the potential for feline altitude sickness, everything seems to catch up with me at once, and I find myself crying on the cotton snow by the manger.

My stomach's full of bile when I wake up sometime later to find Steven leaning over me. There are a few moments when I hope I'm not really awake, that I can dream him here. But his expression tells me this isn't a dream. Well, that and the glittery cotton wedged into my right nostril.

In my head, I think up half a dozen reasons I might be lying here on the floor in the dark, puffy-faced, hours before the pageant. But none of them come out.

Steven doesn't ask. He just joins me on the carpet, picking a stray piece of cotton off the sleeve of my sweater. Maybe the fact that I smell like lemon cleaner and am covered in glitter tells him everything he needs to know.

"I'm glad I found you," he says after what feels like a short eternity. Then he tells me the wise men have started on the eggnog at the inn and compliments me on how shiny the pews are.

He must have turned on the light in the back of the

church. I realize all of a sudden that the windows are dark.

"It's six," he offers.

"Six," I echo. "The pageant..."

"You haven't gone outside. There was a blizzard. *Is* a blizzard." He explains how the pageant's been postponed until Christmas morning so the families who live on the East side of the mountain can get here safely.

I push up onto my knees and start to remove some cotton from my hair.

"We tried to find you," he says. "You weren't home."

"Oh. I was...here," I say. "...early."

He nods. We sit quietly for a couple seconds then, as I try to figure out what to say next. There's nothing to say, really.

"Jeff said you were gone," Steven says just when I'm about to say something about the unexpected weather.

"Jeff?"

Steven nods. "He checked. Inside your office, I mean. I think he was there around noon."

"Oh." Which seems to be the most coherent response I can offer today. *Tonight*. Of course Jeff checked inside my office. He probably came right through the ceiling, the nosy Neanderthal.

"He, uh...seemed to think you might have run away." Steven turns to face me then, and I stop wishing I were asleep and start wishing for everything else, instead.

"You *were* running away," he says.

I start to form some reasonably coherent response

denying this, and it's on the tip of my tongue when everything else comes out, instead.

I don't know how it starts, but somehow, I tell Steven everything—everything he doesn't know already about the investigation, about how I'm probably going to lose my license, or at least not be able to keep my own office, about my needing to find a place where I can work afterwards, maybe at a clinic or an animal shelter under the supervision of another vet, and even about how much I'm liking sticky buns, which are most definitely starting to stick to my thighs.

It comes out in no particular order between little gasps that make me unsure if I'm going to hiccup or throw up.

Then Steven wraps his arms around me, and it just keeps coming out as I lean into him—about holidays and Cracker Barrel and about wanting to stay at this one. And about everything else I've never wanted before now.

I don't know how long it keeps going, but eventually, I'm out of tears and out of words and out of everything else. And then I'm back in the cotton snow, Steven's arms around me, and everything else fades away.

13

I'm in the shower picking stray pieces of cotton from my hair when I hear a "Happy Christmas Eve!" from my waiting room.

I turn off the water. "Beatrice? I'm sorry. I'm in the shower," I tell her through the door, stumbling over the side of the tub.

"I know that, dear, but why?"

I wrap a towel around myself and try to remember where I left my pajama pants. I assume showering's just what you do when you wake up under a Christmas tree with a cardiologist you're falling for, covered in glitter with bits of cotton snow stuck behind your ears and up your nostrils. You walk to your shower—or you skate there along the sidewalk, in my case. It's a good thing I have good hip flexors—and you try to make yourself look like a human being before you return to said cardiologist in the fake snow of the church. Because glitter and cotton are unattractive when improperly applied and all. And maybe a little because I couldn't stop myself from crying. I *still* can't stop, actually. There must be some of kind of psychotrophic chemical in that cotton.

"I just...wanted to shower," I tell the witch in my waiting room. I was hoping it might wash away at least some of the redness. I've caught my breath now, but I'm still pretty red and puffy.

"Annie, dear, please come out," Beatrice says. "I have a delivery for you." She says it like she's trying to talk me off a ledge. And, thinking about it, I'm forced to acknowledge this emotional state, when I'm working towards a lifetime record for longest continuous crying, is probably cause for concern. I think I even cried through my sleep. I'm bound to at least dehydrate soon.

I still can't find my pajama pants, so I dig my onesie out of the box I brought in from my car. I guess it's only appropriate this quiet little haven be invaded by at least one more crazy mountain person while I'm wearing the onesie.

"Oh, dear," Beatrice says when I come out of the bathroom. She says this like someone who doesn't wear multiple scarves wrapped around her head and commune regularly with the great beyond.

The front of the office is still dark, and I glance over at the cat clock I left on the wall. It's only six-forty. I think there's something with the magnetic poles on this mountain that prevent people from keeping normal sleeping hours.

"You can't go back looking like that," Beatrice says, like 'like that' is pretty bad and 'back' is self-explanatory.

"I wasn't going to..."

She raises an eyebrow, and I stop.

"Steven's awake," she announces.

I open my mouth and look down at my onesie. Heat creeps over my cheeks, as though Beatrice might somehow know where I spent the night. And where Steven spent the night. But of course my onesie doesn't betray this information.

I look back at the witch. She's smiling. And she has the kind of smile that could stop a mother hippo, which I'm starting to feel like in the onesie.

"But dear, he doesn't know you just left to take a shower," she says, shaking a manila envelope at me.

"You talked to him? This morning?" I squint into the darkness outside my front window. It hasn't even been morning for very long.

Beatrice shakes her scarves like a macaw ruffling its feathers. "Take these," she orders, pushing the envelope at me. "And go do your hair."

Because it feels like I can't do anything else, I do as she says. The manila envelope goes on the counter, and I go for the hair dryer that was left in the little bathroom cabinet by the last tenant.

I turn it on full blast and feel like the heat must be

frying my brain. It leaves a strange energy buzzing around my ears. But it might not just be the electromagnetic fields; I woke up with the same feeling sometime in the middle of the night. Steven was awake and lying under the Christmas tree like the world's most wonderful present. My head was resting on his arm, which must have fallen asleep much earlier, but he hadn't woken me.

He didn't say anything about the cotton in my nose. He just squeezed my shoulder and told me everything would be all right.

I turn off the hair dryer, and that same warmth washes over me again. It feels like Cola cake on the front porch and late night *Meercat Manor,* the kind of warm fuzzies you want to hold inside you forever. But it's not until I walk out of my bathroom and see Steven in my lobby that they win out.

"Hi," I say, because this is apparently all I can manage right now. I look down at my onesie. I'm pretty sure my face is even more red than when I was using the hair dryer, and now my hair's in something like a fro.

He meets my eyes, avoiding the onesie. "Were you leaving?" he asks.

Beatrice snorts, and she actually *sounds* like a hippo. "Of course she's not leaving," she says.

I open my mouth.

"She's staying."

Steven looks at me, and I can't move. And I guess, for

the time being, Beatrice must be right. The roads are probably impassable all around mountain.

Then, when Steven smiles, warm fuzzies overwhelm my central nervous system, and I swear I taste cinnamon buns that are even better than Coca Cola cake. I look from Beatrice to him.

Jeff chooses this moment to drop in through the ceiling. "Morning," he says, barely glancing at me—the onesie isn't new to him—before turning to Beatrice. "Did you give her the papers?"

"Of course I did." She gestures to the envelope on the counter.

"Papers?" I ask after what feels like a long time.

Beatrice passes it to me. "Your building," she says.

I open the folder.

"This one," Jeff clarifies. "The papers are ownership papers. We got the impression you were probably thinking you couldn't keep the place and run your own business. But that's not gonna be a problem anymore."

Somehow I'm on the floor then. "You're delivering..." I swallow. "A...building?"

"We decided that was the last thing we needed in the settlement," Beatrice tells me, beaming. "You knew the office belonged to Gliel." She crinkles her nose, and I imagine somewhere in Florida, Gliel gets a kidney stone.

Jeff makes a kind of grunt beside her.

"So there it is," Beatrice finishes. "You'll get plenty of

business. And don't worry that detective, or anyone else, is going to give you a spot of trouble up here anymore."

"No," Jeff says. "He won't."

Beatrice takes Jeff's arm and pushes him towards the door. "Now we should get going," she tells him. "She needs to get ready."

I look up at Steven, who's standing on the other side of the counter. Neither of us move.

"For Lucy's," Beatrice prompts. "We can all have breakfast at the inn before you go up the hill. Adam's practicing his pineapple pancakes. You'll want to get ready," she repeats, looking pointedly at my onesie.

But everything, even the onesie, melts away when I look at Steven. He's smiling, and I feel like I'm back under the Christmas tree in the glittery snow and like nothing in the world could possibly be better than this.

"You'll come with me?" he asks. "To Lucy's?"

I laugh. One day, when I'm looking back on it, I'll definitely take the laugh out of this memory. And the onesie.

I don't know what I say to agree or how I find the bathroom to try to fix my hair or even how much hair-fixing gets done, but Steven's waiting for me when I come back out.

"We have plenty of time," he says, reaching for my hand and leading me to the bench in the waiting room. "Jeff's gone ahead to get some coffee while Adam warms up the griddle. I wanted to give you this first."

He holds out a DVD set tied with a green ribbon. It's *Meercat Manor*.

I hear the laugh again and almost don't recognize it as my own.

"I thought we could start a new Christmas tradition," he says. "If you'll...I mean, if you'll spend Christmas with me."

"Of course she will."

I spin around. Beatrice is still here, setting out some Santa dog figurines on my counter.

"This is her first Piney Mountain Christmas," she says.

And there's something about that statement, from the witch who's been hiding in my hallway and intruding on my romantic memory, that I know I'll never forget.

"We can leave Lucy's after lunch if you want," Steven adds. "We don't have to stay long. I mean, she's really not very good around the holidays."

I shake my head, and then we're both smiling. Somehow, today, I know I can face Lucy Lowens. I can face a dozen Olstens. I feel like I can face anything when Steven has my hand.

So I let him keep it. The light from the two flashing reindeer on my rooftop glistens on the pavement outside, and I know this year, I'll be home for Christmas.

Visions of Sugar Cookies

Lauren

The snow that falls on Piney Mountain is unlike snow anywhere else in the world. It floats through the darkness in fat, wet flakes that don't do anything when they hit your windshield, just sort of lazily crystallizing until you drown them with wiper fluid. But you can't kill them. The snow here is fearless.

Chicago snow's different. It's brown, neutralized by the exhaust and broken down by the salt trucks before it ever has a chance of taking hold on the pavement. In Chicago, we travel in taxis like civilized people. But I left civilization about thirty miles from the Roanoke airport.

On the back road leading up the mountain, the snow's a wild thing that swirls around you like an old-fashioned Christmas globe being shaken by a toddler. I fumble with the gearshift of my rental car as I try to remember where the brights are. It's been a few years since I've driven, but the airport's Rent-a-Car counter doesn't ask how often you use your license. Mine, for instance, is primarily for meeting TSA requirements.

The lights of the Piney Falls town square illuminate the last bit of the road, and acid reflux threatens. I haven't had this since I was here the last time, my first Christmas home from college, back in the age of pizza-scarfing and soda-guzzling.

I make a turn away from the town square and up a smaller road towards my sister's house, surprised I still know the way. Behind me, Huntley sighs. His travel cage is buckled into the back seat and covered with blankets to protect him from drafts, but I think it's probably better that he can't see me right now; my parrot jumps to conclusions easily, and he's pretty judgmental for an African Grey.

Lisa's driveway hasn't been cleared of a deep blanket of snow. When I turn in, the hood of my rental car nearly slides into her garage, and then I have to hold onto the railing to pull myself up the steps to her porch. All the lights inside are off, and her front door's locked. Piney Falls must have changed. Or maybe the local bear population's learned how to open doors and raid pantries.

I get that prickly, messed up PH feeling in my stomach again. I pound on the door, but the house is quiet. There's something unsettling about it that makes me feel like I'm in the beginning of a *Supernatural* episode, and not one of the good ones. This is just the setting for a wendigo attack.

I try to shake wendigos from my mind as I walk back to the car. Huntley ruffles his feathers and heaves a louder, more exasperated sigh at me when I get in.

I haven't caught Lisa on the phone since the night she ran her car off the road and ended up in one of Gliel's cabins with a stranger. Of course, now I think that I should have tried calling her more often. But the holidays are my busy season and always a little crazy; people all over Chicago are out gorging on cookies and going on dangerous crash diets. And Lisa's so stable usually.

There are big, round lights draped over Main Street, but the storefronts are all dark, and there aren't any cars outside Faye's place. There aren't any cars anywhere, actually.

I pull at the collar of my turtleneck and turn down the fans blowing heat at my chest. At the end of the square, the biggest evergreen I've ever seen casts a glow out over the lawn.

And that's all it takes for the entire Piney Falls social calendar to pop into my consciousness. It's something about being born on this mountain, I think, like the ability to subsist on lower oxygen levels and the extra stomachs we've evolved with to digest special sugary drinks each holiday. No matter how far we roam, the calendar comes back to us as soon as we get within a certain radius, and we light our windows on the appropriate Tuesday of December and descend upon the Bakeoff and pageant in the days before Christmas the same way the Who's of Whoville all know when the holiday's approaching and go accordingly Wholike. This is a matter of unassailable natural law that feels as old as the mountain itself.

The Tuesday of tree lighting's always followed by sledding at Harker's Christmas tree farm. And as I drive there, Christmas in Piney Falls is all I can think about—not just the tree lighting and the sledding, but the whole first nineteen years of my life. Memories from them come flooding back as I pull off Main Street.

The Christmases I remember best were with Adam. They make me think of hot cider on Harker's sledding hills, of making out behind the orchestra stand and singing in the pageant. I don't remember any Christmases without him; we were inseparable by the time we'd reached middle school. I guess even before that, we were together, racing down the sledding hills and dancing at the new years' parties. Adam and I broke up the Christmas our first year home from different colleges, and I haven't been back to the mountain, or done any Christmas at all, really, since then.

I tell myself it's been fifteen years, and I'm supposed to be wiser, more composed—*older*, at least. Before my flight, I put on my best push-up bra and an extra coat of hairspray like the armor it should be, but I swear I can feel my foundation starting to crack as I pull into the tree farm.

There are lights shining through the front windows of the main house and a warm glow from the skylights in the attic.

I tell Huntley I'll only be a minute and leave the car running.

"Uh oh," he says.

2

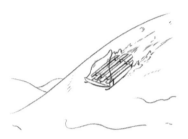

Before I know what's hit me, I'm holding a spiked cider as Beatrice drags me by the elbow through the Harkers' great room. She's commandeered Huntley's cage and put him in the kitchen, where some of the Martins' grandkids have removed his blankets and started feeding him unsalted nuts.

I look around at familiar faces. They all seem to be staring back at me. Beatrice takes me to Jeff first, Adam's best friend since elementary school. He's standing by Faye in front of the fireplace, and they're both looking at me like they've seen a ghost.

Faye snaps out of it first, hugging me and telling me how much she's enjoying the gummy vitamins I sent her.

But when Beatrice mentions I've come to surprise Lisa, Jeff's head jerks up, and Faye looks down at her boots. I've known this Faye gesture since she first foresaw me and Adam kissing under the giant Christmas tree in seventh grade. I was thirteen and livid. I think she was ten. And of course the next year, I was kissing Adam under the giant Christmas tree.

Faye wraps a hand around Jeff's bicep as they explain in starts and stops exactly how my little sister came to be ensconced in a bungalow in Florida with a lawyer until Christmas morning.

As I'm trying to respond to this information, I'm almost knocked over by a gigantic pit bull.

"This is Tuffy," Beatrice informs me serenely as Jeff tries to contain the beast. "He's new."

I look from the dog to Beatrice's face. "Lisa ran off with a...lawyer?" I tell myself my little sister's sensible—a little sensitive to color, but sensible otherwise. I mean, she never showed any proclivity towards running off with lawyers or anything. Obviously, or I would have come sooner.

"He *rescued* her," Beatrice says. "It was all very romantic."

As I think back to Lisa's description of the wreck and the guy in the cabin, I feel the undeniable intestinal discomfort of guilt. I should have asked more questions; had I known my little sister was trapped with a lawyer, I would have done something. Especially if I thought she was thinking of the lawyer in a romantic way. I would have called the police. Or Faye. Or even Jeff.

I look down at the pit bull, who's actually smiling at me, its tongue lolling out as it licks my jeans.

"She hit her head?" I ask. "In the car?" There must have been some central nervous system damage. And she probably wasn't taking her omegas like I told her to prepare her brain for a concussive injury to begin with.

Beatrice pats my arm. "She's going to be very happy, dear," she says.

Some others join us as Faye tries to distract me with an account Lisa's last-minute triumph over the factory and Gliel's banishment. They all look giddy as they describe it, like some mildly psychotic tribe that's just conquered a dictator and is all chummy now drinking eggnog and cider.

This goes on for a while, and I finally manage to pause it with a plea to go to bed. It feels like the jet lag, the altitude, and my past have all caught up with me at once.

"Of course you're tired," Beatrice says, turning to Jeff. "Adam's outside?"

"Adam?" In case any of them were unaware, my voice confirms the state of my digestive system. And here I am, back in this little town just before Christmas with the only person on the planet who can affect my GI without having to feed me anything tainted.

Jeff nods, and Beatrice manages to temporarily distract me with a cream puff one of the Martins is trying for the Bakeoff. I've never let anyone convince me to eat a cream puff before. It must be Adam's presence I can sense nearby. And the tree, and these crazy lighting weeks before Christmas that I never dreaded until they weren't with him. Now there are fifteen years of resentment between us, years which are bound to cause something more serious than intestinal discomfort when we see each other again.

"Adam will take good care of you," Beatrice says.

I look at Faye, who knows very well Adam will do no such thing. She's looking at her boots again.

"You might...if you didn't know," Jeff says, "Adam bought the inn."

I shake my head and feel a migraine coming on. Or at least I think I do; I've only ever had one migraine, and it was from all the crying my last trip down the mountain. "I didn't," I say as my heartburn morphs into what feels like acute cardiac arrest.

I should have known Adam would buy the inn, though. That was always our plan, until that year, to move to Mt. Airy, North Carolina and open a little bed and breakfast together in the setting of Andy Griffith's Mayberry. How appropriate Adam would get the only inn that mattered to me, instead, the one I grew up in.

When we came back for Christmas our first year of college, Adam was at Indiana on a freshman year baseball scholarship and planning on joining me at UNC afterwards to study hospitality management. That

Christmas was when he announced he was switching his major to marketing and staying at IU.

"He left marketing after just a couple semesters and went to pastry school," Beatrice adds. "It's funny, isn't it? You were kind of living parallel lives all along."

Parallel. I guess she means like Jeckyll and Hyde. "I'll...stay at Lisa's," I say.

"Don't be silly," says the psychic with a blue snowflake scarf anchoring a pair of antlers to her head.

"No," Jeff says.

I meet his eyes, because facing even Jeff is better than having to face my first ex-boyfriend.

"I can't stay in my sister's house?" I fish my cell phone out of my coat pocket. "As soon as she checks her messages, I'm sure she'll say..."

Jane, the local writer, approaches and gives me a hug, telling me my new jeans are some sort of tribute to men's breeches in some British king's court, probably in hopes of confusing me into submission. This is how Jane usually gets by.

"I'm sorry," she adds, about the Lisa's home situation. "She gave Jeff the key."

I can see why Jane would be sorry about this. "Lisa will say I can..." I start, but Jane's shaking her head.

"We left the final settlement offer locked up at her place, and it has to stay confidential until it's gone through. After the holidays."

"But you could open it for me." I look from Jane to Jeff, who serve on the town council with my crazy little sister. "You could move the papers, take them somewhere else, and..."

Jeff shakes his head. "I told her I'd keep it locked up," he says. "Sorry." And he looks like he might actually be a little sorry. But probably for Adam, not for me.

"Adam will be so surprised," Beatrice adds, of the man responsible for my future ulcer. Probably for all of my ulcers. I get the feeling I'm going to have a lot of them.

"I'll text him that you need a room," Faye says. "Give him a heads up. You haven't been home in such a long time, it'll be such a...surprise. A good surprise." For all her otherworldly powers, Faye's always been a shitty liar.

"Fifteen years," Jane clarifies. "It's been fifteen years."

"Right. Thanks," I add.

"Adam has the snowmobile at the end of the sledding route," Jeff tells me. "He'll take you back and get you settled."

"Thanks," I repeat, with enough stomach acid making its way into my vocal folds that I'm not sure he hears the sarcasm.

Beatrice nudges me towards the door. "I'll bring your bird on my way back into town," she says. "Don't worry. We'll make sure he stays warm and happy."

They herd me across the porch, and a blast of cold air nearly knocks me over. Jeff hands me a sled as his pit bull laps at my boots like some sort of deranged, toothy zombie.

I'm pretty sure the music *Supernatural* plays just before a demon appears sounds like the cold and the trees and the laughter of the kids at the bottom of the hill. *Fifteen years.*

The sides of the sled fit more snugly around my backside than I remember as I sit down. I push off with my new suede boots, and my weight makes me skid even faster than the kids on the snow.

As I get closer to Adam and the discovery of just how much Christmas bile is left between us, I feel like the Grinch descending on Whoville.

3

The next morning, I wake up in the old town inn with a face all the serums in the world couldn't help. My forehead's red and bumpy like a sunburnt lizard.

Huntley at least seems to have fared better through the night. When I went to bed, I left him napping on top of his travel cage so full of nuts and bits of gingerbread that he turned his beak up at his organic sunflower seeds. Then, this morning, he made a noise that sounded almost like a meow while I was doing my makeup. I guess the mountain air affects African Greys, too.

I manage to wait until I can see Adam's truck's gone before hunger forces me out of my room, and I'm engulfed in a bear hug as soon as I step into the kitchen hallway.

Kevin, Adam's not-so-little-anymore little brother, has

given me the same kind of heimlich hugs since he was a quarter of his current size. He's twenty-one now and knocks the air out of me.

He still calls me Renny, though. It brings back those days for me, laughing over board games on dark winter afternoons and playing tag through the spring wildflowers. It took me and Adam a few years to teach Kevin my real name, and then he thought we were related until he was six. He was still young when I came home the last time—too young, I guess, to hold a grudge.

"Adam said you wouldn't eat sticky buns." And that's the first thing he says to me. I guess it sums up everything that's happened in the interim pretty well.

As we catch up on the last fifteen years, I see he's still the same Kevin I remember, with his short sentences and his big, toothy smile and his gorgeous singing voice. He tells me he got a music scholarship to West Virginia and started playing guitar, too—just a little, he says, but he's probably a star. Kevin was a kind of accidental child prodigy who was more interested in cookie dough than in music. Beatrice discovered him when he was just five, Adam's and my last Christmas in high school, when he first sang in the pageant.

Now, he's excited for me to try his first attempt at making eggnog.

I look at the list of ingredients on the sticky note he's holding. "Brandy *and* rum? And two and a half inches of heavy cream," I read. The rest of it's mostly sugar.

"It's cold in the mountains," Kevin reminds me. "It helps to have a little extra fat in your booze."

He pours me a cup as I feel the zit on my forehead starting to gain altitude. There's just too much of my past in this kitchen. More of it's good than bad, of course, but it's part of a group of memories I've sworn off, of a life I've left behind.

So I turn my thoughts to acne-preventing fruits, instead, as I sip the eggnog. It tastes like whipped cream and nutmeg. "You don't have any papaya, do you?" I ask.

"What?"

"Papaya. A fruit." I wonder if papaya's ever seen Piney Falls. The general store probably only has pinecones this time of year.

"We have pineapple," Kevin offers before opening a closet which is, in fact, filled with pineapples.

I gawk. It's like a fruit mirage in a desert of lard.

"It's one of Adam's things," Kevin tells me. "He has this big new year's luau every year."

I cut off a chunk of pineapple and rub it across my forehead as Kevin tells me about an aloha soup recipe and a pineapple martini Adam's planning to make this year.

"I can give you a sample," he offers. "He's been making up a little batch each day, trying them out."

I shake my head, probably too enthusiastically. But

there's no way either aloha soup or a pineapple martini would go down right now. "I'm really just here for some quinoa," I say.

"What?"

"Quinoa. It's a grain." I fish a little baggie out of my purse and hold it up for his inspection.

Kevin stares. Not that I had much hope. This is the kid who used to eat whole sticks of butter.

"You just have to boil it," I tell him. "It's a complete protein."

He looks at me like I've just suggested it's a complete pineapple martini. "There are a lot of vegetables," he says, "if that helps."

I follow him to the inn's pantry, the haven of the canned vegetables. It's not like anything grows up here. I'm pretty sure the community started as a cargo cult. That's how I've always imagined the days of our grandparents, anyway, the town ritually slaughtering a yule log every now and then in hopes of a good Christmas tree growing season and a storm of canned tomatoes.

But Kevin bypasses the pantry and goes to the refrigerator, instead. Miraculously, it's filled with green stuffs, this one like a cruciferous mirage in a desert of white flour. I open a drawer with some broccoli and kale. *Kale*, for goodness sake. I didn't even think Adam knew what kale was. Maybe I'm hallucinating from a sudden lack of fiber or something.

"There's some kind of organic co-op growing all that

on the way down to Radford," Kevin says.

An organic co-op. And here I was expecting pinecones. But Piney Mountain's always full of surprises around the holidays.

"There's not much more broccoli," Kevin warns, "but you'll keep getting squash and leeks and yams for the next couple months."

"I won't be here for a couple months," I say automatically.

Kevin's lip curls, and I see in him some flash of Adam. It's the smirk. Kevin's skin is a shade lighter than his brother's, and he has sweet brown eyes that crease up in the corners, all laughter and dimples and teasing. Whereas Adam's eyes are see-straight-through-you, bottomless pools of ink.

"So you want your sandwich instead of..." He frowns at my quinoa baggie. "...that stuff?"

I agree and am surprised to find a whole shelf of fresh tomatoes when he opens another refrigerator. Lisa refers to the sandwich as my contribution to the mountain. I was seven when I asked Eddie Lowens, the inn's original owner, to make me a grilled cheese with some tomatoes inside, and I guess it caught on.

My brain tells me I shouldn't think about this time or about Adam, especially right now. But my voice betrays me. "Does Adam serve these? The sandwich, I mean?"

"Yeah, sure," Kevin says, adding some olive oil to the

bread and turning on the griddle.

A gulp of Kevin's eggnog gets stuck in my throat. Literally stuck. There's that much cream in it. "Really?" I ask. When I last saw him, Adam's diet consisted primarily of roast beef sandwiches and cinnamon sticky buns that never seemed to stick to him. Maybe he's forgotten this sandwich was mine.

I slice a tomato as Kevin tells me about the pageant this year, which Eddie's nephew, Steven, is directing with the assistance of the town's new vet, and I wonder what schemes Beatrice is cooking up. Kevin was too young to remember the brightest final days of Beatrice's public psychicdom, but she was like a supernova just before it explodes. Now she's concentrated her psychicness on the mountain. I think of this like concentrating ammonia, only you can't smell it coming.

I steam a few stalks of broccoli as Kevin's finishing toasting the bread and regaling me with tales of Adam's new flying Star of David. The broccoli's tender and doesn't take long, and doing this reminds me of Eddie teaching me how to steam vegetables on this stove when I was nine. Lisa told me his wife, Lucy, turned evil when he passed away, but I can still feel his warm presence all over the kitchen, welcoming and friendly. It was Eddie who helped me decide to pick the best school for me, too, who told me not to worry. Everything was supposed to work out in the end.

When Kevin and I sit down and I bite into the sandwich I haven't had for fifteen years, I can still smell Eddie's homemade bread and see him standing over the big wooden counter in the middle of the room.

Kevin asks if I still cook, and I tell him about the wonders of Whole Foods and their freshly-prepared meals, instead. Today, though, I'm wondering why Whole Foods can't make a grilled cheese this good.

4

By my third day on the mountain, I'm clutching garlic like I'm trying to ward off the Volturi and taking my sublingual B formulation like there's a nationwide shortage of folate. Day three also finds me in the inn's kitchen with Kevin and the Piney Falls knitting club for their annual Bakeoff practice.

Lucy, Eddie's widow and Beatrice's long-standing runner-up with her lady fingers, grins at Kevin's lemon bar mixture over his shoulder as she kneads some dough. It's the last practice round of the Piney Mountain Bakeoff, the last day for experimenting. Tensions are high, at least for Lucy.

I look over Kevin's other shoulder when he tells me his starter isn't frothing right. He's whisking something that smells like lemon Pledge in a metal bowl.

"Can you help get it foamy?" he asks.

I tell him I'm not very qualified with respect to lemon foam, which is the truth. That, and I've never measured the success of food items by their degree of frothiness.

"Come on," he says. "It's vitamin C, isn't it?"

I glance over at his recipe, which is written in what looks like Adam's scribble on a piece of copy paper. It's mostly sugar. At least it's not aspartame or high fructose corn syrup. I guess that's something.

"You came down here to get involved, didn't you?" Kevin presses.

"Uh," I say, mostly to the lemon bar mixture. "Not really." I just wanted some broccoli.

But Kevin doesn't budge. "Beatrice said you'd want to get involved," he says, waving a hand over the bowl and wafting lemon smell my way. "She was finishing up this morning when I came down, and she said you'd be here soon."

Of course she did. The witch must get some signal from the great beyond whenever I need broccoli.

"And Adam..."

I don't hear much of the rest. I turn my attention to beating at Kevin's bowl with a whisk as the ladies of the town take turns glancing at me and making faces at each other. Kevin, apparently oblivious, keeps talking about his brother, and I commit to chronic indigestion.

My problem with Adam isn't really in our past or in

some great logistical problem with us seeing each other again, like being trapped at the inn together until Lisa gets home. There are dozens of exes I could be trapped at an inn with and not develop an ulcer.

The problem is something chemical, this strange pull he has over me that's more powerful than dark chocolate and shortbreads and Christmas combined. Adam's like my own brand of MSG; every emotion I experience is more intense with him, and some part of my brain's tricked by the neurotoxin to seek him out again and again, thank goodness usually just in my memories, to try to work through what happened between us.

Kevin's lemon bar mixture has millions of tiny, foamy bubbles, and even he seems a little intimidated by my whisking abilities when Adam himself walks into the kitchen. Then spatulas are dropped, bowls left unattended as the knitting club ladies gather around him with rapid-fire comments, questions, and cookies.

He looks thin. His new haircut makes him look like Taye Diggs. Did he have it done at that new place in Radford? Has he tried both varieties of lady fingers yet? Does he like the powdered sugar coating on the gingerbread cookies? Does he think the pineapple complements the pecan puffs?

"Don't you think Lauren should make something for the Bakeoff?" That one comes from Kevin.

The ladies all fall silent and turn to face me. I stare at

Adam, who looks like a chipmunk with his cheeks shoved full of gingerbread and lady fingers. But it's his eyes, like always, that stop the laugh in my throat.

I swallow. "I was just here for some…" 'Broccoli' makes me sound like such a food prude. "I just wanted to say hello and….wish everyone luck," I finish weakly.

Lucy Lowens sniffs. "She's probably never made cookies. She'd try to add tomatoes."

The other ladies chuckle as the evil one grins at her clever vegetable reference. She's like the ringleader of a bunch of geriatric playground bullies. I hope Jane and Angela get here soon. They at least pretend not to judge me for my tomatoes.

"She cooks loads of stuff for her clients, don't you, Renny?" Kevin asks, apparently unintimidated. "She just taught me how to steam things yesterday."

Adam meets my eyes, and I can actually feel another zit forming on the tip of my nose. At this rate, I expect I'll spend Christmas looking like Rudolph in his teenage years.

"I'm not really much of a cook," I say, mostly to my sweater, because I can't hold eye contact any longer. "And since I'm not from here…I mean, since I'm not…here." I stop, because I don't know what I mean. And, you know, because all the blood in my body's rushing to my nose.

"There are no strangers in Piney Falls," Kevin faithfully repeats the town slogan.

I nod at my sweater, but I'm feeling a lot like one. And, when I look back at Adam, I remember I'm looking at one, too. This isn't the boy I drove away from fifteen years ago.

"The Bakeoff's open to anybody," he says after a second. "Doubt I'd have what you need, though. Don't you make everything with rice flour or something now?"

My face heats up as the ladies titter.

"I'm not gluten free," I tell him. Obviously, or I wouldn't still eat grilled cheese with tomatoes. At least not grilled on wheat bread. But Adam knows this, knows more about me than I'd like him to. And I'm frozen here, looking at him and seeing everything he was before *we* weren't anymore, when I say that I *do* want some rice flour.

It takes me a second to realize I've said it. I don't know where it came from, and with so much venom. And *rice flour*. I don't even like rice flour. But he probably doesn't have any cassava.

"You're gonna cook?" Adam's voice is loud, the way I hear him so often in my head when I'm trying to sleep.

I look around the kitchen, at all the faces of the knitting club ladies who have stopped pretending to be busy with their own cookies. Lucy purses her lips. It's too late to back down now. "Sure," I say, shrugging as casually as I can. My shoulders get stuck in the *up* position.

Adam opens a cabinet and hands me a baking sheet and a bowl. He doesn't look at me as he turns to leave.

"Don't you make something?" I ask his back.

The ladies of the knitting club simultaneously lower their heads. Even Lucy turns away to knead quietly at her dough.

I turn away, too, when I hear his exhale. If he were a cartoon character, I think smoke would be coming out of his ears.

I keep this observation to myself as I claim the workstation by Kevin's. But I know Adam's still there behind me, probably wishing me off a cliff or at least far, far away from this mountain. I stall for a while, wandering around picking out random ingredients that aren't broccoli and cauliflower, before the ladies start looking back at him.

And then Adam has his own mixing bowl and is smashing around in the cabinets.

"What's that about?" I ask Kevin when Adam finally steps out of the kitchen and my heart returns to a normal rhythm. "He finished school as a pastry chef, didn't he? You'd think he'd be giving Beatrice a run for her money."

"I don't know," Kevin says. "It's been a while, though." He smiles, and his eyes go all fuzzy like Adam's used to. "I've been craving those cream puffs he used to make."

Eventually, Adam stomps back into the kitchen and drops a giant bag of rice flower—where he got it, I have no idea—at my workstation. Then he grins, and I feel acid burning the back of my throat before he even opens his mouth.

"I almost forgot," he says. "Beatrice wants to see you."

5

That evening, Adam and I find ourselves on the same side of an argument for the first time in fifteen years.

I thought getting involved in the Bakeoff was a simple matter of...well, of baking. I had no idea forces were conspiring to get me involved in the pageant, too. Powerful forces. Unnatural forces. The forces Beatrice commands.

I've dealt with off-the-rails nutritional clients and hordes of entitled businessmen and suppliers in some of Chicago's roughest neighborhoods, but Beatrice is another story. And she's in three scarf mode tonight. With two, she's unstoppable. With three, she's like a psychic typhoon.

"Lauren doesn't want to be here," Adam reminds her. I don't think it's occurred to him yet that he's on my side of this. "She probably won't even come to the pageant. Once Lisa gets home and the litigation's out of the way..."

"The litigation won't be out of the way until after Christmas," Beatrice whispers.

This is how it started, with a whisper—an ominous whisper that she was losing her voice and wouldn't be able to sing the angel's part this year. So now Faye's wearing giant, sparkling wings and preparing to be an opera singer, and apparently I'm the last person on the mountain who can play the mother of Christ. Angela's already leading the fairies, and Jane's the narrator and would probably rewrite the part of the angel to give it some sort of literary edge if given the option to trade.

"And Lisa won't be home until Christmas day," Beatrice adds.

"But Lauren's a terrible actress," Adam says.

Of course he's right, since he's playing Joseph. Fifteen years ago, most of the town saw our last performance as a couple.

"She's perfect." Beatrice's voice comes out suspiciously normal, in its usual foreboding way. Then she clears her throat and starts up a purple rhinestone-clad ipad, and I have the sudden urge to force feed her elderberry.

Adam waves his arms like a disgruntled pterodactyl. I think he's gotten taller. "The virgin Mary? You're saying Lauren is perfect to play *the virgin Mary*?"

Beatrice's ipad says *Yes.*

"She's bad with kids. She'll make the baby cry."

Beatrice flips over her ipad and starts typing again. *Not a problem,* she writes. *We're using Puffy.*

Adam rolls his eyes, and I wonder what a Puffy is. On Piney Mountain, it's probably a rabid hamster. It seems to me the new vet would be a more appropriate choice to hold it, whatever it is, but she's co-directing the pageant with Steven. And darn Beatrice for not seeing fit to pair me with the cardiologist for her Christmas matchmaking. A *cardiologist,* for heaven's sake, and Eddie's nephew to boot.

Out of options, I offer her every trick I have for warding off a cold, the flu, and all manner of sore throats, but nothing can thwart a Beatrice in three scarf mode. So within ten minutes, I'm wearing a long blue dress-sheet.

As Adam keeps trying to reason with Beatrice, or at least with Beatrice's ipad, I spot Faye, the great stomping archangel of Piney Mountain. She's downing a giant mug of coffee and pacing in front of the stained glass windows on the far side of the church.

When I join her there, she greets me with a wave of her mug. Her jaw's clenched, and she looks like she's had enough coffee to turn an elephant into a show jumping horse, but otherwise, she's glowing. And not just from anger. Based on the way she's chugging the coffee, it's not from beta carotene from juicing carrots like I recommended, either. And I know she doesn't swallow pills. Which leaves only one likely cause.

"So, you and Jeff," I start.

She stops stomping. She smiles. She blushes. She's in love with a friggin caveman.

"It's still early," she tells me. But whatever *it* is doesn't look early at all. She looks like she's had some sort of oxytocin overdose.

She's not the only one in this state. I think it's something about environmental exposure, maybe some kind of radiation up here, but it seems like people are coupling up everywhere in the church, blushing and flirting and being generally infectious. I recall the Tanganyika "laughter epidemic" that made about a thousand people temporarily nutty in Tanzania in the sixties. This is just like that, I think, only with hand holding, and I don't see any flatulence, fainting, respiratory issues, or rashes. So probably less contagion than Beatrice at work.

"That's...great," I say.

"Are you staying?" she asks. "I mean after Christmas. Beatrice said you were doing some school nutrition stuff."

"What?" I want tell Beatrice's gummy vitamin-guzzling grand-niece that she's wrong, but Beatrice is kind of like Cinderella's fairy godmother meets the psychic mafia.

Faye frowns. "Maybe I misunderstood," she says, but I can see from her face that she didn't misunderstand anything. My best hope is that she got her witchy wires crossed.

"That's what you're working with, though, isn't it?" she asks. "Schools?"

"Most of my clients are individuals," I tell her. "But I'd like to. I mean, I've been wanting to for a while. Have you heard of pink slime?"

Faye studies me for a second in a way that almost convinces me *I'm* the one with the temporary psychosis. "Our school lunches come from the inn now," she says. "You knew that, didn't you?"

I gape at her, but no words come out. I can't imagine Adam supplying children with sustenance. He's probably arming the little monsters with sticky buns.

"You know Radford, the counties around here, are terrible," Faye continues. "Virginia was like second to last in school lunches nationally, and the mountain areas are the worst. You can't get vegetables here as cheaply as you can somewhere that has trucks coming in every day."

I nod vacantly. So that explains all the vegetables at the inn. "Adam's cooking with vegetables now?" I ask.

"He started a few years back."

"Does he...um, eat them?" I shouldn't ask, I know, but it's Adam, the pastry chef, the bane of any nutritionist's existence. And mine especially.

Before she has a chance to answer, Faye turns roughly the color of a ripe tomato, and I see Jeff approaching. He usually makes a lot of noise when he walks, more like a gorilla than like a panther, but I guess his boots deaden the sound. Specifically *these* boots, white lace-ups peeking out from under purple crushed velvet bell bottoms. He's also wearing a magenta silk shirt covered in orange flowers.

When he gets to us, he holds out a pomeranian to me like the wise men offer the gold, frankincense, and mhyrr.

"What's this?" Its little arms are outstretched, its tongue lolling to one side.

"Puffy." Jeff says it like I should know this, like pomeranians routinely accompany Mary to deliver the savior of mankind. I take the dog, which is actually much smaller and lighter than it looks under all its hair, and it promptly hides its head in my armpit.

"He's the baby Jesus," Faye explains.

I look down at the slightly vibrating Christ child nestling into my sweater. "I birth a...a pomeranian?"

Jeff nods, and I try not read anything into this. Mainly because I don't know a lot about scripture other than what it says about complete proteins in ancient grains.

A few minutes later, he points me and Faye to the backstage area, and we go to opposite sides of the wings to take our places. While I'm waiting, I get some advice about swaddling Puffy from the little fairies and angels, who are currently dressing up Jeff's pit bull in a pink tutu. One of the fairies promises she'll tell me when to go on stage, giving me leave to retreat deeper into the empty hallway at the side of the church.

I watch through a window as Jeff discos his way across the stage when "Jesus Christ, Superstar" starts up. The speakers are booming, and the wall vibrates a little.

My nose twitches. I sat with a chunk of pineapple on it for half an hour before I left the inn, but my zit's undeterred. The whole area's starting to turn red now, and the bump's growing like a staph cyst. I can feel it just under the surface, ready to pop out and greet the world, probably right when the Christ dog makes his appearance.

I look down, and Puffy licks my chin, sitting up on my forearm to see the show. Just when I'm starting to be impressed by Jeff's dancing—he's always struck me as more of a Frankenstein type—the disco ball plummets to the floor and rolls down the stairs to the center aisle. One of the wise men dives into a pew, and everything shuts down for a few minutes as the stage is flooded by cast members and cookie-makers alike.

The rest of the first act is a little less eventful, at least from an OSHA standpoint. Jeff's pit bull interrupts the Eid feast, tail wagging as he's chased by a pack of angels while he prances across the stage in his tutu, and then one of the presents takes off in cartwheels and rolls down the stairs of the apse, but it's high entertainment of the quirky sort, like if the original cast of the Bible were all high one night and got together with some Muslims, Jews, and Pagans for a big, friendly brownie party.

Then Adam appears at the end of the hallway, and

nothing feels friendly at all.

"What are you doing?" he asks when he sees me.

I clutch Puffy a little tighter to my chest, and it occurs to me I'd rather face a *quadruple*-scarved Beatrice than Adam. But I have as much right to be hiding in the hallway as he does—more, maybe, for being an outsider who was bullied into being here in the first place.

"I was waiting. Watching," I correct. *Enjoying the show* would have been better, I guess. *Producing excess stomach acid in preparation for the moment we walk out on stage as the most famous couple of all time* is probably more accurate.

He looks at me like he used to look at my special grilled cheese sandwich before he'd get his roast beef.

"I usually wait here," he says.

"I was here first." I meet his eyes, then turn away. We should be beyond this. There shouldn't be a *we*. *I* should be beyond this.

Puffy looks up at me, and I try to focus on the window again. This is about how Adam and I interacted early on in elementary school. And maybe it's safest to revert, since what happened between then and now didn't go so well for either of us. Or at least for me. Adam looks no worse for wear.

He takes a step forward, and I hold my ground and clutch the pomeranian a little tighter.

"You've changed," he says.

"I haven't changed at all," I tell him, and it comes out

about as bitter as we both should have expected it to. Because I wasn't the one to change my mind about Mt. Airy or anything else.

I remind myself people are supposed to grow up a lot between nineteen and thirty-four. Our cells have turned over twice; there's nothing the same about either of us. So it doesn't make sense he should still affect me like this. We really are different people now.

Adam takes another step closer and somehow in my subconscious morphs into what he's always been, a neurotoxin, my MSG, tricking my brain into thinking it's hungry when it's full, making me crave more, like rats who have that cat fecal parasite that causes toxoplasmosis are drawn back to the host even though they know they'll be eaten.

He shakes his head, probably sending more neurotoxin my way. In some ways, I guess it's true that I haven't changed, even if I have on a cellular level; I probably still would have disagreed with him if he'd said I wasn't a grilled cheese sandwich.

"Look," he says. "We're gonna have to get through this."

Vaguely, I know there's music out in the church, a pageant rehearsal going on, little angels dancing around with a pit bull, giggling and singing through mouths full of Christmas cookies. But I can't hear any of it.

"Can we call a truce or something?" Adam asks, "and

forget about...about everything, I guess? Just until after Christmas?"

I nod, but I know I'm not doing any forgetting. Not here. Probably not anywhere, ever.

He keeps talking, trying to make this comfortable somehow, and I guess I keep responding, at least a little, about the play and about the inn and about pineapple casserole, which I'd think would elicit a more memorable response on my part. And then he's humming.

"A truce," he says. "You get it?" He's holding out his hand, and mine moves as though compelled to shake it. Obviously, I don't get anything.

He grasps my hand and threads my fingers through his as he starts to sing the lyrics from Eddie Lowens' favorite album. His hand's warm, and his voice goes straight through me, like it always has, hurtling me back into who I used to be. There's no music now but his.

Our hands remember each other like I knew they would. My feet shuffle, and when I close my eyes, I can hear Alabama singing "Tonight is Christmas" through the clanging of pans in the kitchen on the scratchy old tape player Eddie used to keep in the corner. I know these lyrics by heart, this beautiful moment when Christmas pauses a war.

I think Faye should be starting her solo out on stage around now, but I don't hear it. I'm lost, again, in Adam, like I have been so many times before.

He keeps my hand when he stops humming. I guess we're predisposed to this somehow. Past life issues, Faye would say. Beatrice would probably call it destiny. Our chests collide, and Puffy lets out a yelp.

6

The kitchens are overrun by nine the next morning for the final round of the Bakeoff. Flour's flying. The ovens are all on, leaking heat and high levels of radiation through the ground floor of the inn. Most of the knitting club has stripped to strappy undershirts as they toil over their cookies. It's not pretty.

Lucy Lowens squints at me as I hurry to my little workstation by Kevin, whose lemon bar mixture has experienced an unexpected resurgence in frothiness this morning.

"I used some of your agave nectar," he tells me.

I guess I should have seen this coming. The world really is turning on its head on Piney Mountain. Huntley spent half the night meowing.

Lucy's stopped her batter-beating and is watching us, apparently threatened by Kevin's lemon bars. That, or she's spotted my nose, which sprouted a zit this morning that's too bright for the toughest concealer known to Sephoraites. I may as well be leading a sleigh.

As I get some baking supplies from the cabinet overhead, Kevin tells me Adam's constructing something in the big refrigerator down the hall.

Maybe it's thinking about Adam as much as it is the heat, but it's not long before I've sweat off all the powder on my nose. My dough isn't rolling right today, and I'm pushed to add more agave nectar. I look over at Kevin, who's making a kind of tower with his lemon bars.

"It's an ice castle," he tells me.

I bend to study his creation. It looks like a very gooey, very powdery Jenga game.

While he arranges the lemon bars, Kevin explains how the Bakeoff competition escalated this year, fostering a paradigm shift away from mere taste and towards the ridiculous and the colorful. It started with Lucy Lowens who, I guess slowly losing her mind getting second place year after year, began fashioning her lady fingers to be more lifelike, complete with knuckles and long, festively-painted fingernails, in a desperate attempt to overthrow Beatrice's reign of shortbreads.

I look around at the other participants, who have begun to roll their dough into Christmas-themed shapes, breaking out the sprinkles and colored frostings.

I spend a while trying to form my dough into a three-dimensional snowman, because that's all I can think of to make with a blob of gluten-free sugar cookie. After about another half hour, I have an armless body that looks like anemic elephant poop.

"Wait a minute," Kevin says, stepping back from his lemon castle to examine my snowman's middle. "These are gluten free, aren't they?"

"Right."

"What if we teamed up? You know, made one big, gluten free...winter scene?"

I warn him I don't really know how to cook this. There's no precedent I'm aware of for cooking through a snowman's middle. I was planning on giving some to Puffy as a peace offering.

"It's okay," Kevin assures me. "Adam has a special red light oven that cooks from the inside out."

This doesn't seem possible, but I decide I'm willing to bend the laws of physics for now. My headless snowman's already taller than Kevin's castle, but maybe having the extra moral support of a partner will help. Anyway, Lucy's looking threatened as we start to combine our work, and I like it.

By ten, my snowman's cooked through at least enough for me to deem it safe to eat, since it was made with free range eggs, and I'm rolling smaller, gumdrop-shaped cookies for the tasters to sample for around the base of our little winter community. Kevin's mixing cream cheese frosting with powdered sugar to make some snow drifts and an ice skating rink, and Lucy's face is reddening by the minute.

I've sweat off all traces of my makeup by the time the taster cookies are finished and off to the oven.

Just as Adam leaves in search of some strawberries to top his castle and I'm wishing I'd reapplied some powder, Adam emerges from the big refrigerator down the hall. I swear he'd smell like MSG if it had an odor, and I feel his presence turning the rest of my face as red as my nose.

He doesn't comment on my face and instead says something vaguely complimentary about my frosting ice skating rink, I guess trying to keep our pact to be nice to each other and forget about the last fifteen years, or maybe about the last twenty years, or maybe we should go back twenty-five or thirty, to be safe, until after Christmas.

He starts sorting tiny red and green sprinkle balls at Kevin's empty workstation, and I try to distract myself with the cream cheese frosting. Which isn't easy when you're 95% dairy free.

But over the next half hour, I outdo myself. I'm digging snow angels in powdered sugar in an attempt to preserve my sanity when the giant cuckoo clock over the door strikes eleven.

Adam's drawn white icing designs around the edges of delicate little sheets of puff pastry. They're the kind of mesmerizing geometrics you'd see in mandalas, adorned at the corners with little colored balls in reds and greens.

"You're an artist now," I say.

He shrugs. "I learned at school," he says. Then he points to my sheet. "Is that edible?"

"It's cream cheese," I tell him, but it comes out uncertain.

Adam comes closer to look, and I can actually feel my nose zit gaining altitude. It keeps growing, and we keep talking, right up until Jeff bursts through the door with the pit bull.

7

A pit bull in a kitchen full of Bakeoff cookies is even worse than an ordinary bull in a china shop, but he's nothing compared to Jeff. Jeff looks like a wendigo who's just woken up from his fourteen years of slumber and is ready to go snatch some innocent campers from the woods. I step in front of my workstation to shield our winter scene in case he's bent on pastry destruction, too.

It doesn't help that he's followed closely by a scarved Beatrice, for the first time in a way I can't count because she hasn't folded them neatly over her ears in little pashmina layers. I can only assume this indicates the beginning of the end of the world.

"That awful Olsten's coming," she tells us, waving a hand at Adam, who evidently takes the disarray of her scarves in the same way I do. He abandons his swans.

Beatrice's purple outer scarf is encased in snow, and she starts unwrapping to reveal a red layer underneath. "I don't know how he got up the hill," she says, "but he'll be here soon. We'll have to try and feed him."

Adam's already across the kitchen and attempting to lure the pit bull into a storage closet, and Beatrice takes this opportunity to catch me up on the pit bull-Olsten situation. Evidently, Olsten's a ghastly rent-a-cop from Radford, and he's come looking for Annie's pit bull, which he suspects, rightly, is here, and has not been euthanized, as Annie claimed, before she left New York. Apparently this euthanization was court-ordered. So, for reasons I'm probably not destined to understand, we're harboring some sort of man-eating fugitive.

"But we don't want to worry Annie," Beatrice says. "She'd be very upset. She's in the church."

"Uh...huh," I say.

When Jeff gets back from the hallway, there's a loud crash, and the beast reemerges from the closet.

"Olsten came up the back road?" Adam asks. "In this?"

My thoughts haven't strayed from the kitchen all morning to notice any inclement weather. I glance out at the dining area, but I can't see the windows. At least it's not ice. We would have heard ice coming down even from in here.

But we didn't hear Olsten. I know who he is as soon as he rounds the corner. His pinched face looks like it's started to crystallize with snow.

Beatrice opens her mouth and for a second just stares at him. I've never seen her speechless before. But she recovers quickly.

"Officer Olsten!" She waves a jeweled hand around the kitchen like she's showing off a brand new car on *Wheel of Fortune*. "We were just finishing the final round of the Bakeoff. You'll want to try some…"

But Olsten's staring at the pit bull, whose tail is thumping noisily against the cabinets under Jane's empty workstation.

"What's *that?*"

We all turn to look at the dog as though he's just materialized there.

And I don't know what comes over me then, if it's the smug look on Olsten's face or the fact that he's refusing some perfectly good peanut butter cookies of Angela's, or if I'm accidentally channeling some of Jeff's wendigoness.

"He's mine." My voice comes out louder than I expected. I turn to face the monster, who's drooling prodigiously after lapping up some spilled flour. I walk over and pat him on the head. His tail continues thumping against the cabinets.

Olsten squints at me. "*Yours?*" he asks. And suddenly, I'm with Beatrice in wanting to stuff his smug face full of cookies. Or, better yet, something with trans fats and aspartame so metabolic acidosis can haunt him for the rest of his days.

"Mine," I confirm. "His name's...Chia." I must be missing my little chia pods from Whole Foods.

Beatrice grins, and some more of Chia's drool falls to the floor. I notice that Chia has very big fangs.

"Lauren's come to visit her sister for the holidays," Beatrice says. "She's living in Chicago for now."

I don't even blink at the "for now" as I meet Olsten's eyes again.

He crosses his arms over his chest. "So when'd you get in?"

"Just at the beginning of the week," Adam offers. "She booked Chia here and her parrot in advance."

Olsten looks at Adam, then back at the dog. I kneel beside Chia and ruffle his ears. Now he looks sort of like a giant rabid bat.

"Doesn't Chicago have some kinda ordinance about pit bulls?"

"I'm not in the city limits." It comes out before Olsten's closed his mouth.

The beast licks my face. Olsten glares, and then I definitely pick up some of Jeff's wendigo energy.

"Is there a problem? Because we're very busy today, what with the Bakeoff." I listen to myself in Piney Mountain accent and all. It's like someone else speaking from inside my body.

Color's rising in Olsten's face. He's clearly lacking in Omega 3's. "I need to talk to Dr. Norton," he says. "*Alone*."

Beatrice shakes her head. "I'm so sorry. We had to send Annie out on an important errand, and she won't be back for some time."

Adam nods. "Yeah. We needed more sticky bun dough."

Olsten just stands there staring at the dog before sputtering, "He's...in the...kitchen."

His color makes me think he's going to have a heart attack. He has a sweat mustache now. I wonder if there's a hospital close enough we could get him to. Or if we would, or if we'd just bury him.

"...the...health code."

"Oh, not at all." I must be powered by some sort of angry association between the officer and the FDA. He's wearing one of those ridiculous little yellow badges on his coat and everything. "He's my therapy dog."

"Your..."

"Therapy dog. I have panic attacks. I could get you the documentation," I offer when Olsten doesn't move.

Beatrice smiles serenely at him. "Why...you didn't think that *he* was the dog Annie euthanized come back to life, did you?"

Olsten turns to face her but doesn't manage to get out any words.

"No. No, I'm sure you didn't," she continues, "because

we all know Chia here."

Adam nods robotically. I look at Jeff, who hasn't taken his eyes off Olsten.

"We sure do appreciate you coming up in all this weather, and right before the holidays. We weren't expecting you," Beatrice says. "It's a shame Adam's out of rooms this weekend, but you should stay for some hot chocolate, at least, before you head back to town." She takes Olsten's elbow and tugs him out of the kitchen. Chia whines.

"No," Olsten says.

"What about a to-go cup?" Beatrice asks.

He opens his mouth like a goldfish and turns back to me. I'm betting on a myocardial infarction before he even gets to the back road. And that's if Jeff doesn't get to him first.

"I'll drive ahead with the plow, clear for you to the dropoff," Adam offers. Because we wouldn't want the bastard to get in a wreck or anything, sneaking up the mountain trying to catch a pit bull and destroy our new vet like this. *Our new vet.* There it is again, like I'm one of them. It must be the electromagnetic radiation from the ovens.

Jeff steps forward, and Olsten stumbles, bumping into a dining table. Jeff's clearly having other ideas about the dropoff.

Probably wisely, Olsten says something about needing to catch up on some paperwork and refuses any escort down the mountain.

Adam walks to the window to watch him drive away, and Beatrice congratulates me on my quick thinking as the toothy beast in our midst engages in some celebratory agave nectar from the counter.

"Oh, look at that!" Beatrice says, gesturing to Eddie's old cuckoo clock over the doorway. "It's time to go to the refrigerator."

We form a little processional of cookie sheets, and Beatrice coos over Kevin's and my creation even as the castle starts to droop and a strawberry slides sideways over a turret.

Lucy's painted lady fingers are already on a shelf surrounded by three layers of protective plastic, and one corner of the room is taken up by Adam's giant cream swan with the gorgeous designs on its wings. It's flanked on either side by a handful of smaller swans, a little family. I study them as the rest of the contestants leave and Beatrice goes over supply needs for the evening with Adam. She pats his arm when she turns from the room, assuring him she'll take care of the music.

"What about the pageant?" I ask. "Isn't it tonight?"

She waves a dismissive scarf at the dining area, where people are starting to trickle in. "There's a blizzard," she says. "Make yourself comfortable, dear."

With that, she leaves us alone, and I realize just how uncomfortable a refrigerator is in December, and with Adam in it. I fiddle with some plastic wrap over my ice skating rink, then try to bolster Kevin's lemon tower for a few minutes before turning to leave, but my stomach's already spewing acid. And Adam's still standing in the doorway.

"Why'd you do that?" he asks when I have to turn his way.

"What?" I want to walk past him, to leave all this behind us, but I can't seem to move my feet.

He gestures to the kitchen. "The dog. Say he was yours."

"I..." And I don't know what's going to come out next. "I didn't want the vet to get in trouble...or the dog to be put down. He seems..." *Rabid.* "...nice," I finish. He went straight for the agave nectar when it was unattended, which at least bodes well for the beast's judgment. And it's so much easier to think about a frothing pit bull than to think about Adam and every part of myself I've left here on this mountain.

I read somewhere that you're supposed to get over someone in twice the length of the relationship. So if you only count the time we were dating, I should have been over Adam in fourteen years, last year. But my thoughts definitely stayed with him. If you add these years together and I stop thinking about him right this moment, I should get over him in forty-four years.

"But you don't care," Adam says. "You don't even know Annie."

"Olsten's a pompous ass. And it didn't sound like he was in the right, the way Beatrice explained it." Maybe that's all it needed to be, I tell myself, that I'm just a good person who would normally look out for strangers and enjoy thwarting bad governmental enforcement. But it wasn't so much latent anger at the FDA as it was a general kind of protectiveness for the mountain. Piney Falls residents have a tendency to stick together, no matter how far away we go or how much farther we *should* go.

"But this isn't where you want to be," Adam says. There's a breath between us, then, that feels too long. "Is it?"

I think I'm about to answer when he makes a face, turning to the hallway.

"Hang on," he says, and calls for Beatrice to come back.

I wonder when I'll have to answer him. Beatrice says questions, once they're out in the universe, don't just disappear.

She materializes instantly in the doorway.

"Where are your cookies?" Adam asks.

I glance around the storage room, but sure enough, there are no magical shortbreads in sight.

"Oh dear," Beatrice says. "I absolutely forgot." We follow her to the kitchen, where Jeff and the dog are busy devouring everyone's scraps.

Beatrice opens one of the old ovens in a corner, and a roll of smoke billows out and up towards the rafters. When it clears, I can see blackened little drops on the sheet. I half expect a phoenix to rise from the ashes.

"Lucy's gonna die," Jeff says from behind me. I'm pretty sure he means of happiness, but he sounds hopeful.

Beatrice shrugs. "Well, I guess that's that," she says, closing the oven and turning to Jeff. "You go now and get Faye. And someone will need to give Lucy a ride here before the snow picks up. Steven's busy, and she can't stay in that big house by herself if the power goes. I know she wanted a fair competition, but I was just so worried about the dog, I forgot all about my shortbreads."

None of us move as she saunters casually out of the kitchen.

8

A few hours later, the impromptu party's in full swing, the pageant having been successfully postponed. The Bakeoff entries are all safely locked in the refrigerator since the tasting's been put on hold, too. I think only Piney Falls could reschedule a community event for Christmas morning and expect a full house. Beatrice says it being the first morning pageant makes it special, like a Christ pomeranian and a flying Star of David might not have made it special enough.

Kevin returns to the kitchen, where I'm finishing mashing some guacamole (because apparently, the greater Piney Falls community has strong feelings about pre-Christmas steamed broccoli). He grabs a spoon to sample it before I can offer him a tortilla chip.

A guitar starts tuning out by the fireplace, and Kevin tells me the college students who are here for the holidays have been set loose for musical entertainment, no doubt Beatrice's work. I think Beatrice's work is probably even more extensive than is immediately apparent.

I offer to watch the food rather than venture out into the open and tell myself this is necessary now there's a hungry pit bull loose in the inn and my holiday truce with Adam's a fragile one. I'm not sure how good we were at keeping peace between us even when we were in different states, so it seems safest to at least keep one wall between us now.

Kevin takes the trays out, and I pull out a barstool. They're new, but they're a solid, well-worn oak Eddie might have picked out himself. When I take a bite of my special sandwich, it tastes like wonder and Christmas. Better than carrot juice. Better than *brie*, even. And I can't believe I'm thinking about brie now.

The band in the dining area sounds a little wobbly, but I can hear Kevin's sweet voice drifting in through the doorway. He sings some traditional stuff and, even though it couldn't be farther from Alabama's "Tender Tennessee Christmas," it takes me back to the holidays I actually celebrated, to the part of my life I've spent the last fifteen years trying to bury in work and the bustle of the city. My real holidays were all here, of course, at the inn for Christmas breakfast and scattered around town for parties in the weeks before, sledding and tree lighting.

I start to sway, and soon, I'm dancing like I did when I was seven, twirling around the kitchens with Eddie's broom before I crashed into Lucy's first ever Bakeoff lady fingers, and like I did in the pageant as a little angel, and then as a fairy. Not so much like I did with Adam every year from age fourteen to nineteen.

But my twirling this time is more dangerous than the one that landed me in Lucy's lady fingers; this time, I come to a stop facing Adam.

We stand there frozen until the song ends, and I don't know why I feel like I have to explain myself. He walked into *my* memory, after all, and the man in front of me now isn't the boy who was a part of it.

"We have a truce," I remind him, as though anyone needs any more remembering in this kitchen.

"Yeah, I..." Adam gestures to the dining area, then drops his hand as he turns back to me. "So you made guacamole?"

He makes it sound like a question, like there might be someone else on this mountain who makes guacamole. I don't even know what he was doing with avocados here. But I guess I don't know a lot of what's happened in the last fifteen years.

"You had a lot of avocados." It comes out defensive.

He holds his hands out in front of his chest. "No. No, it's good, I mean," he says. "They like it. I was coming to get some more."

I feel my face flush.

"Don't you want..." His voice trails off as he turns back to the doorway. "I mean, you should go out to the party."

"It's okay," I tell him. "I'd rather stay here."

He nods, getting more avocados out of the refrigerator across the kitchen. When he comes back and sets them out on the counter, I wish we'd made our truce a little more specific. Forgetting about everything that's happened in the last couple decades probably requires some clause about our proximity. Then again, a couple thousand miles wasn't far enough away for me, so I guess I shouldn't expect a brick wall or two to do the trick now.

We start mashing and cutting and chopping, and our conversation comes naturally despite all the awkwardness that should be between us and all the stomach acid that's at least getting me. As far back as I can remember, things have always been this way with Adam. We keep talking even though we both know we shouldn't.

Our conversation covers everything from the president to the Bulls. We don't mention careers or exes or Christmas, and as we discuss the merits of expanded cable coming to the mountain, I try to pretend this isn't what I've felt like was missing from all my dinner conversations, and from everything else, for the last decade and a half.

I've heard there's something to this pattern, some

theory that we never really get over our first loves. They establish a kind of bar that creeps up on us and sets a standard for butterflies and attachment and wonder that no subsequent relationship can ever live up to. I guess this is why talking with Adam is doing what it's always done to the back of my brain. It leaves the rest of my faculties all but paralyzed when it should be spewing cortisol, even though now he's just talking about the makeshift band of college students Beatrice arranged in the dining room and how they're eating their weight in sticky buns.

"Are you going to make any more pastries?" I ask. I guess it's only appropriate my cognitive malfunction becomes apparent with talk of pastries. "Regularly, I mean."

Adam stops mashing the avocado and looks at me.

"I haven't been," he says.

I stare down into the green mush, trying to channel the front of my brain to override everything going on in the back. "The swans were...great," it says anyway.

"You had one?"

"I thought we had to wait for the tasting. I meant that they're really pretty."

Adam sets down his fork. "*You're* gonna eat a white chocolate puff pastry swan?"

My stomach actually rumbles. His eyebrows are all crinkled, like they were when we first tried to swing dance in sixth grade gym class and, somehow, my elbowing him in the face surprised him.

"You, uh...remember what a pastry is, right?" he asks.

"I do." But my voice comes out hoarse. Like the last time I was home for Christmas, probably from too much screaming and crying that time.

I turn back to the bowl and try to ignore his presence a couple steps away, distracting myself by stabbing at some onion chunks.

"You're serious," he says.

And there's nothing I can do about it. I don't know when I've ever been anything but serious about anything. Especially where Adam's concerned.

"You're gonna eat a pastry," he repeats.

"I'd try one. You should make them more often." This is just going to keep getting worse. "You could even make them healthier," I say, "or with agave nectar, or for people with allergies, like gluten free."

I wish Beatrice or something even more destructive would appear now to interrupt us. We've already had a blizzard. Maybe a tornado would do it, I think. But nothing comes, and so we're just here, together, with the Christmas music wafting in through the doorway.

After the swing dance incident of our junior year, you wouldn't have guessed it would be Christmas music that did us in. But it does. Adam and I are dancing in the kitchen when the music slows down, Kevin's voice crooning a sweet rendition of "I'll Be Home for

Christmas."

"Thanks, by the way," Adam says. "For the guacamole."

His breath's warm against my cheek, and I nod, beyond articulation now. I close my eyes, glad he can't see my face. This is one of those tricky things about Christmas—our conception of the holiday is set by our strongest memories, the traditions and the people who mean the most to us, even when these are the people we most want to forget.

It's too warm in here for how cold it is outside. I'm too close to the ovens, and to Adam. And then not close enough. My arms wind around his neck on their own, and he runs a hand over my back while his other wraps around my waist.

Then the song winds down, and for some reason, he has to talk.

"Why didn't you come back?" His hands go slack at my waist, and he takes a step away. "For fifteen years, Lauren. Why didn't you come back?"

I open my mouth, and I don't know what it's going to say before he stops me.

"I'm sorry." He pulls me closer again as the band segues into another song. "I am. Forget that I asked. Please."

And then my arms are around his neck again, my face buried in his shoulder. I know the answer, have known, probably, since I was fourteen. This was self-preservation, all these years, knowing I would fall apart if I saw him again. I don't want to think about how this is just a temporary truce and it will all go back to normal—and I'll go back to Chicago—as soon as Christmas is over.

And maybe someday I'll say this was all inevitable, that this is what Beatrice means when she talks about fate and why fighting it doesn't get us anywhere. My stomach has something like butterflies, but big and strong, more dangerous than candida and SIBO put together.

When the music changes again, Adam brings up our truce. "We can fight, talk about it, whatever, right after Christmas," he says.

I swallow. "After Christmas," I agree. Then we're kissing, and I don't remember the butterflies ever being this good.

9

The next morning, my lips feel like I've downed a bag of Celtic sea salt, and my face has a topography like the Glens of Antrim. Since this week's the first time I've had acne since I was seventeen, when I first discovered the power of hyaluronic acid and thyme extract, I guess I shouldn't be surprised Christmas Eve day finds me making vegan banana cake drizzled with cocoa sauce.

Kevin's absentmindedly stirring his fourth batch of eggnog beside me as he bemoans the perils of college-age dating. Beatrice has launched a mission to set him up with Lucy Lowens the younger, named for her grandmother. He thinks Lucy Lowens the younger is pretty nice. They're fairly simple perils that plague college-aged males around Christmastime.

He leans on the edge of the counter and inhales some eggnog steam as he waxes philosophical about why we try to find partners at all when we're happy in other areas of our lives.

I don't know how to respond. But then, I'm older, less wise. It's seems like there's some evolutionary quirk that makes us go crazy, even when everything else in our lives is perfectly hunky dory, over someone who will only mess it up and give us acne and ulcers. Somehow, *who* the back brain wants always seems to win out over *what* the front brain chooses.

My banana cake's almost solidified when I pull it from the oven and try a little piece that's flaked off the side. The cocoa sauce takes me back to hot chocolate on the sledding hills at Harker's and kissing Adam by the giant Christmas tree in the town square. But then, most everything does now. I think the kiss last night made those memories more intense. So maybe it's right that I'm gorging on coca-drizzled banana cake after having its pheromonal equivalent.

When Kevin goes back to his flirting in the dining room, I take another piece of pineapple up to my room in hopes of thwarting the acne mountain taking over my nose. No amount of makeup and magical city serums are sufficient preparation for a Piney Falls Christmas eve, especially here at the inn. I turn on the TV for some noise before I start my shower.

The bathrooms here are the same pink-tiled

sanctuaries I remember and smell like the gardenia sachets in the drawers. The tiles are covered in condensation before the shower's even warm. Some goat milk lotions from a farm a little ways past Radford are lined up along the shelf by the medicine cabinet, and I focus for a while on reading their ingredient lists.

I can hear Christmas music from the kitchen radio through a vent in the floor, and when I dry off and come out in my robe, Huntley's sitting on top of his cage watching a romantic movie on the movie channel, which I guess ran out of *Home Alones* this late in the day. While my hair's drying, I sit on the bed and join him for a few minutes of calm before the party starts downstairs.

It's one of those movies that had to keep going past Christmas and into spring, like there wasn't enough mistletoe around Manhattan in December for the story to end there. I think some romances are like that, though, taking their time when they should be wrapping up. It's at that optimistic almost-end like all the good ones have, the dreaming-of-a-relationship stage before anything's solidified.

That part's the best one, I think, when anything's possible and you just take the possibilities you prefer—this career, that location, this lifestyle, that variety of yogurt, *not* those in-laws. When you're dreaming about possibilities, you don't have to think about compromises, about the dream trading markets of real life.

I stop the movie where I think it should end and finish drying my hair with the little blow dryer from under the sink. When the TV goes dark, Huntley meows mournfully. Maybe he knows he'll be missing Mrs. Martin's gingerbreads soon, or maybe he can tell what this trip's already done to my sanity. The fact that he's learned how to meow at all is probably red flag enough for both of us.

As I'm pulling on my leggings for dinner, my eyes are drawn back to the little yellow notepad on the dresser. It has the phone number of the Radford area schools' superintendent Beatrice has already talked to about my consultation services.

Beatrice has a funny way of identifying dreams from miles away. Before I told her, she knew I was more interested in pink slime in schools than in love handles on socialites. But this is what you do, if you don't have a meddling psychic in your life; you talk yourself out of things, committing to smaller dreams, and sometimes just sticking to dreaming itself.

Beatrice might also be the only other person who knows that facing Adam, that coming back here and staying at the inn and birthing a pomeranian and baking a giant, gluten free snowman, is the biggest risk I've taken in a long time. I look in the mirror and try to see some difference in myself, some indication that I have a new intestinal fortitude, at least, a fearless microbiome that will leave me a different person at the end of this week.

My reflection doesn't look fearless, though. My reflection looks a little like Bloody Mary from that creepy episode of *Supernatural*. I'm one of those unlucky people whose hair and skin reflect emotional health, and my face currently resembles the inside of an anemic pumpkin.

I sit in front of the mirror for a while trying to compensate with more BB cream, but I'm still missing all the glowiness carrots and calm and Chicago can provide. I cake on two more layers of concealer before I work up the guts to go downstairs.

10

The first round of Kevin's eggnog's almost finished by the time I get to the dining room. The college kids are singing carols at the piano, and I wonder where their own holiday traditions and their families are now. I didn't get all of their stories, but I know somehow, Piney Falls will be part of their conception of what Christmas is forever.

Most of the rest of the community's tucked into booths or standing around the hallways eating cookies or warm sticky buns. Kevin, who seems most interested in after-dinner sledding with the younger Lucy Lowens, sings beautifully even when he forgets some of the words to "Good King Wenceslas."

Beatrice gives the toast before dinner, rather smugly prophesying we'll all become braver and wiser this coming year and raising her glass to the season of hope and joy. She talks about love, too, but not in the sappy, happy way you'd expect to hear about around the holidays; her love's the real one, the kind of chaotic joy that encourages ulcers, bilial sludge, and pancreatitis.

The college kids are grinning and making cow eyes at everything from each other to the banana cake by the time we're through dinner, and as I study the scene from the kitchen doorway, I think this must be the kind of Christmas Eve you'd see in a painting, alternating between caroling and sledding under the stars, snow shoeing and laughter. But it's better than a Norman Rockwell, even, more real. There are old ornaments mixed in with the new ones on the tree, and the college students use way too much cocoa on my banana bread, giant blobs that look like polka dots. The white lights on the mantle don't match the colorful ones around the windows. The stockings are all a little lopsided.

When I take some dessert dishes away, I notice Kevin's third pot of eggnog's almost gone, and suddenly that I'm overheating, like I've eaten too much cinnamon. I think it's my body re-remembering who I am and where I am at once.

I nip up to my room with the intention of huffing whatever lavender facial spray I still have left to get the evergreen out of my nose and Adam out of my head. But there's only so much lavender can do. And even if I OD'd on valerian and eggnog now and went to bed, I know my dreams would get me.

And then Adam walks into the room. Because this door has probably never been locked, and I didn't have the foresight to bury myself in a snow bank with a hospitable bear until the holiday's over.

He tells me that he knocked, which some part of my brain probably heard. He thought I'd be here, he says, and figured I might want some hot chocolate.

I wipe a few drops of lavender spray from the edge of the dresser and close a drawer filled with all the makeup that will never be good enough to cover my face here.

When I look at Adam, I know I'll never leave this room, in some part of my memory. I'll just keep coming back here over and over. Maybe in another forty-four years, when I should finally be getting over him, I'll wonder if I made the right decision in walking out of it. Maybe I'll think about what my life would have been like if I'd been able to make a different decision now, or if I'd come back to Piney Falls under different circumstances years earlier, or if Lisa were home and I'd never ended up in this room with Adam at all.

He tells me the college kids have taken off with sleds for Christmas Eve romance in the snow. Beatrice is gone, too, off to meet Faye and Jeff at his cabin for a late dinner. Everyone else on the mountain's tucked in with eggnog or hot chocolate and a fire.

These things with Adam are, of course, the Christmas

I know I can't have, and my stomach lining tells me everything I need to know about my ability to walk away from this one unscathed.

So I try to do what I know works, to fight about something. Anything at all. Because at least I know how that ends, with slammed doors and yelling and walking away. I don't know what happens now if we don't fight or how many more lifetimes it will take me to even start to get over it.

I try for what feels like a short eternity to start the fight that should save us this, but it just doesn't take. Adam lets me talk for a while, damning everything from the Bakeoff to the ice and blaming Beatrice for most everything and him for the kiss, which I immediately regret mentioning. When I've run out of breath, he walks over and wraps his arms around me.

My hands fist on his chest. I should have had more eggnog. I think it might have at least helped to dull this. But Adam's arms are around me, these arms I know so well, and then there's nothing else.

"We're not fighting tonight," he says.

He runs a hand down my hair, and my forehead goes instinctively to his shoulder. Then we're sitting on the bed, on an old pink quilt made by Beatrice's grandmother and probably cursed with something just as powerful as this thing that lives between us.

"The day after tomorrow," he tells me, "you can say

whatever you want. If you have to leave then, fine. But not tonight."

I can't leave, because I can't move, and I can't fight, because I can't talk. So I'm just here, now.

11

Christmas is white and persistent on Piney Mountain—like its snow, but with even more spirit. Sunlight streaks in triumphantly through the windows of the church, and big bursts of evergreen scent billow up around the town center from the tree farm and the preserve.

The church was packed at least an hour before Jeff boogied his way across the stage, the pews bustling with Bakeoff cookies and laughter and last-minute stocking exchanges. Now the fairies are backstage playing with a new remote-controlled helicopter found under one of their trees, and the angels are running around with a tutu-clad, tiarra-wearing pit bull.

Before the pageant started, Beatrice announced the results of the Bakeoff voting. It was a close race, she told everyone, and one which for the first time merited three separate categories. Adam's swans were a clear winner for the brand new artistic baking award, Lucy's lady fingers won the overall taste prize, and Kevin's and my gluten-free snow scene won the community contribution to baking award. It was almost as good as winning a silver spoon for my cauliflower leek recipe. Actually, it was better. But it was a funny morning that winning a new category of the Piney Mountain Bakeoff wasn't what stood out.

I guess nothing was going to top waking up next to Adam for the first time. That's the thing about living in the same town; you always end up in different places, and then, when you least expect it, fifteen years later, you fall asleep on top of the covers after talking all night.

I took a different place in the wings today to watch the opening scenes, leaving Adam to his hallway. But I'm feeling the neurotoxins even more now, probably magnified by Christmas and the pageant and being dressed as the mother of the Christ pomeranian.

I thought for a while this morning, when I snuck down to the kitchen in the dark and binged on cocoa-drizzled oatmeal, that it was just because it's my first real Christmas in such a long time. I'd hoped the feeling might fade after I'd had some fiber, but it turned out to be something about Piney Falls and about Adam and about *home* that even cocoa-drizzled oatmeal couldn't pull me out of.

I think I probably knew it before I watched the

stocking exchanges, with Dr. Steven Lowens playing Santa and Chia in his reindeer antlers licking all the kids' faces for their Christmas portraits. Probably before Beatrice told me the investigation on Chia—*Tuffy*, Jeff was quick to remind me—has been abandoned. Probably even before the mountain's most powerful matchmaking witch handed me the school menus for Radford in my not-so-newly-sewn, personalized stocking. Probably even before I got on the plane, I knew this place is home.

I look across the stage as Adam, having successfully guided the disco ball back into the wings, retreats to his hallway to pace. I can see the top of his head pass by the little window every couple minutes.

I came to the church straight from breakfast. I let Angela do my makeup in the sacristy and even sat through Jane lecturing me on the origins of the Hebrew words in the script rather than go back to face him. I think I didn't want to ruin the moment, or something like that, when I woke up. And I was drooling, and I knew all the concealer had rubbed off my nose. And I didn't know what to say and was afraid whatever he might have said then wouldn't have been what I wanted to hear.

It's a funny thing, fear, that's strongest around the holidays, too. I thought I was pretty immune—I got through leaving Adam that Christmas when I was nineteen. I changed my major. I braved the big city. I even drove a rental car up the friggin mountain. But it was always there.

Before the rest of the cast got to the church, I left a voicemail for Radford's superintendent to say I'll start working on their menus for next school year.

Lisa and her lawyer will be here in a few hours, just in time to catch the after-party at the inn, and then I'll tell her that my trip back to Chicago will be a temporary one this time. I still don't know how I'll tell Adam, and I wish I had Puffy with me, or anything else to focus on as our scene gets closer.

My stomach seizes up when I see my cue, Adam coming towards the little, poinsettia-lined road we take to the stable.

Faye's fluttering around in her angel wings across the stage as she gets ready for her song, now accompanied by Kevin.

I reach out for Adam's hand. This time, I keep it.

Jane narrates our journey to Bethlehem in English, and then again in Hebrew, for good measure, and I don't mind the delay. Adam squeezes my hand, and I finally look up into the audience when I knock on the innkeeper's door.

My eyes settle on the grinning witch in the front row, and I have a feeling this Christmas is going to end exactly as Beatrice planned it.

Epilogue

January arrives with a glistening coat of snow and a hardier eggnog recipe from Kevin to sustain us through the darkest months of winter.

The pineapple—both on my face and in virtually all of my food for the last few days—finally took out my zit by New Year's morning, and I started the year with a restoration of sense and a glass of carrot juice with some lemon. For now, Adam's procured a mini juicer for me from Radford, Faye's started using my carrot pulp in her muffins, and I'm looking forward to bringing the first Vitamix to Piney Falls as soon as UPS can get it up the mountain.

It just shows how much can change over a Piney Falls holiday. This morning, I guess thinking I hadn't changed enough for the both of us, Huntley greeted the new year by purring. Kevin said it was probably some acoustic effect of the Hawaiian music he'd heard through the walls. Adam thought he was imitating my snoring. Beatrice was certain he got it from Mr. Jingles, a cat who passed away over fifty years ago and who liked to follow around couples, playing matchmaker. Faye turned green on hearing this and has been babbling about snowball demons ever since.

In addition to setting loose a matchmaking ghost cat, Beatrice recorded this year's pageant in both video and audio formats, no doubt beginning a tradition and starting a collection we'll want to forget for years to come.

New year's eve was more traditional, except for the pineapples, and Beatrice got a recording of Kevin singing "Auld Lang Sang"—a surprise especially to Kevin—that's playing through some speakers at the side of the field now.

It's cold out in the middle of the snow-covered site Helsein cleared before they were run out of town by my little sister and her new lawyer. But there's something about a Piney Mountain holiday that chases away the frostbite.

The new Piney Falls community center will boast a giant stone fireplace, an art room for an after-school program Faye's heading, a special needs room, complete with our first special education teacher, some rooms for tutors to use, and a book club area for Jane outside the new lecture and performance hall. Lucy Lowens is getting her soccer fields, too, and Jeff promises the center's special bamboo floors will hold up so well to her grandkids' dirt that he needn't demean his profession by building anything called a "mud area."

He's helped design a giant blue windmill that will be visible all the way from the base of the mountain and a compost geothermal unit that will supplement the energy grid. Sourcing the labor and materials locally will leave enough of Heslein's money to spare for a large community fund and a scholarship program. The old town hall, a relic of what will henceforth be known as the Gliel Age, is slated to become a recycling center because, as Beatrice put it, no mayor of ours is going to need an office.

Now the cleared area around the transplanted Christmas tree has been roped off with a big blue ribbon, and a circle of onlookers, consisting of most all of the surrounding community, has quieted down.

I lean into Adam as Beatrice steps up to the microphone and offers a blessing on the land. I think it starts out in English, but then it morphs into something else entirely, some ancient language that belongs to the mountain, and my eyes well up when Lisa, Jane, and Jeff cut the ribbon.

There's lots of cheering when the ribbon flutters down to the snow and the crowd disperses back to the tent to pick up plates of pineapple-themed leftovers from last night. I take a seat in front of a little space heater and watch them all while I wait for Adam.

Annie's sipping hot cocoa with Steven, who's promised to do regular health classes once the little lecture and performance hall is ready. Jeff and Faye are sitting next to them with Chia/Tuffy. Lisa waves back at me as she jogs towards her car. My little sister hasn't been able to contain herself since she discovered she has not one, but two new structures in town to decorate. She immediately decided my cabin needs a sunroom. Her lawyer's chasing after her with a box full of gingerbread cookies, looking totally out of his element and totally in love.

I shade my eyes from the sun reflecting off the snow, smiling when I see Adam watching me over the pineapple casserole.

He opens his mouth like he's going to say something derogatory about my soon-to-arrive Vitamix and its pulpy creations, then evidently thinks better of it. His new year's resolution is to stop saying things he shouldn't. Mine's to stop my ulcer. I think I've been doing pretty well since Christmas.

"You know we could go to Carolina," he says. "We could drive out and see what it's like this spring."

But this time, my stomach knows right away that some plans are better off forgotten. Even Mount Airy can't hold a candle to pineapple casserole in the snow.

I shake my head and go kiss him, and it's better than

any I remember. Piney Mountain beats Mayberry any day
of the year.

CPSIA information can be obtained
at www.ICGtesting.com
Printed in the USA
LVHW040951071221
705486LV00001B/22